Wake Me at MIDNIGHT

Wake Me at MIDNIGHT

Barthe DeClements

SCHOLASTIC INC.
New York Toronto London Auckland Sydney

ACKNOWLEDGMENTS: I wish to thank my son, Christopher Greimes, and my daughters, Nicole Southard and Mari De-Clements, for their work on the manuscript. I wish to thank Kris Kellogg and her students at Benjamin Rush for sharing their activities with me and to thank my son Roger DeClements for unknowingly contributing his laconic manner of communication to the character of Bones.   B.D.

ISBN 0-590-45444-7

12 11 10 9 8 7 6 5 4 3   3 4 5 6 7 8/9

Printed in the U.S.A.   40

First Scholastic printing, September 1993

This book is dedicated to

my niece, Michele,

and my nephews,

Jim, John, Mark, and Ralph.

1

I STARED into the dark room, holding my head above the pillow to hear the strange noise. Was someone digging? At midnight?

Creeping out of my bed, I put on my slippers and padded across the room to the French doors which opened onto the deck. The sound stopped abruptly when I stepped outside. Ohh. I'd better be quiet.

I waited silently. Except for the soft patter of rain, the night around me was still. I waited. And waited. Was that the shape of a person by the Reddings' back fence? The white fence glowed faintly in the dark and it seemed as if a hooded figure was crouched in front of it. Leaning on a shovel?

A long time went by with nothing happening and I wished I'd gone to the bathroom before I'd come outdoors. Then the dark shape moved. Down and up. Down and up. Someone *was* digging! I couldn't see the ground, but I could hear the scratch of a shovel sliding into dirt and see the swing of arms throwing the dirt aside. Why would anyone be digging in the middle of the night?

Was it Bones? Or his mother? Bones is thirteen and about the same size as his mom. But the motions weren't quick like Bones's are. Maybe he was wearing the hooded blue rain-jacket that hung inside the Reddings' kitchen door. That would slow him down.

Still, I couldn't even be positive it was the blue jacket because all I could see was a dark, pointed shape. My curiosity won out over the rain and I kneeled down to crawl toward the far edge of the deck, hoping the railing would give me cover. At the edge, I squatted on my heels and peered through the rails.

The view would be better nearer the corner, I decided, so I scooted over about four feet. *Clunk. Crrack!* One of Mom's flower pots had taken a dive through the railing and landed on the cement. I froze.

A light flashed from the figure and the beam searched along the edge of the deck and down to the patio below. I crooked my neck to hide my head behind the planter. My body was pasted so flat to the wet floorboards I could feel each nail.

The beam came up and went along the deck again. It went back down to the cement. Then it went off. Total darkness. I waited. The person must have waited, too, because there was a long silence before I heard the *chunk, chunk, chunk* of the shovel again.

I stayed motionless for a few minutes longer and then scooted backwards until my feet hit the doorjamb. Getting up, I slipped inside the French doors and shut them quietly. Close call.

After I'd gone to the bathroom and changed my soaked pajamas, I climbed back in bed and wondered why I'd gotten so scared. It was only the neighbor. I would have felt stupid, though, if I'd been caught spying. What would I have said?

Bones was the kind of guy who kept himself private. Even ninth graders backed off when Bones gave them his cold, level stare. And I was just a sixth grade girl.

I drifted off to sleep thinking of the chocolate chip cookies I'd baked that afternoon. I planned to take a sack of them to school and casually share them with Bones. I was always careful never to mention how starved he looked.

I must have been asleep an hour when I woke up again. It was Jimmy. His buggy was in the hall right beside Mom's room. I lay in bed a while, hoping she would get up and take care of him. No such luck. I dragged myself out from under the covers, put my slippers back on, and fumbled my way downstairs.

By the time I got to Jimmy, he was howling. "There, there," I cooed. "Caitlin's here. Caitlin will take care of Jimmy."

I unwound him from his blanket and took his soaking little self into the kitchen. After I'd put his formula on to warm, I undid his diapers and swished the bottom half of him under the faucet. Mom was in her bedroom snoring, so she couldn't yell at me for washing him in the kitchen sink.

She never snored before she had Jimmy. I think it's a signal to Dad and me that she's too tired to take care of the baby. And since Dad's gone three weeks out of every month, guess who gets to do it?

When the bottle was warm and Jimmy was in dry diapers, I carried him upstairs to my bed. He'd been spending the last half of his nights with me for two months. Mom stayed home with him for four weeks after he was born and then decided it was time to get back to her job.

She'd hated, hated, hated having a baby when she was forty-three years old. She felt like a fool in the hospital because the new mother who roomed with her was twenty years old. The same age as my sister, Susan.

I hated, hated, hated hearing this. Especially since

4

Jimmy's little and helpless. And smells delicious. Not when his pants are full or when he's spit up, but all the rest of the time.

Tiny puppies smell good, too. When my collie, Germaine, was alive I used to let her out of the pen so I could steal one of her puppies. I'd lie on the couch with it, petting its soft fur while it slept curled around my neck.

Now that Jimmy was three months old, he wasn't always ready to curl up and sleep. After he finished his bottle, he thought it was playtime. "Come on, Jimmy," I coaxed. "It's almost one o'clock in the morning."

I settled on my back and wrapped my arms around him. He waved his arms and legs like a starfish, trying to claw his way off my chest. I fell asleep hoping he wouldn't learn to crawl before he stopped waking at night.

The babysitter came at eight o'clock. Mom was drinking her coffee in the kitchen while I hovered by our front door. As soon as I heard Bones's back door slam, I was down our porch steps. I made it to the sidewalk just as Bones came around his house.

I stuffed half a cookie in my mouth and held out the sack to him. He hesitated. I chomped on my cookie as if I cared less if he had any. He reached in the sack and took one. "Take two," I said.

He did.

When we'd walked half a block, I asked him, "Are they good?"

"Sure. They're okay."

I shifted my book bag to my left arm and held the sack out again. "Have some more."

"Naw, that's enough." Bones was never going to admit he was hungry.

"It was weird last night." I was saying this slowly, not certain how far I should go. "Some strange noises were coming from your yard."

"So? What kind of noises?"

"Like someone digging."

"You're wacko."

"No, I'm not. I got up to look and someone was in your backyard all right."

"You mean a dog." This was the way Bones usually talked when he thought I was exaggerating.

"No! Not a dog," I said, sure now it hadn't been him I'd seen. "It was a person. When they heard me, they turned on a flashlight."

"Then what happened?"

"Nothing. I ducked out of sight. After a while, whoever it was went back to digging and I went in the house."

"What time was this?"

"Midnight."

"You were dreaming."

"No, I wasn't!" But I'd lost his attention. He was focused on the Dorman brothers who were getting out of their car across the street. Bones's dark gray eyes narrowed as he watched them tug at something heavy in the backseat.

"How come Bob and Derek always put a blanket over the stuff they bring home?" I asked.

Bones didn't answer me.

"And how come Bob makes Derek carry everything? Because he's the youngest?"

"No, because he's the stupidest." Bones continued on down the street and I trotted after him.

I felt he knew something about the Dormans I didn't know. It would be useless to ask him any more questions, though. If I did, he'd get irritated and not talk to me at all. I searched around in my head for something interesting to say. I couldn't think of anything.

The closer we got to the schools, the more kids we bumped into. If the girls didn't know Bones very well, they called him Paul. The guys who only knew him in classes called him Redding.

Just before we reached the junior high, I gave my book bag to Bones and took off my sweater. He stood impatiently on the sidewalk while I pulled down each sleeve of my T-shirt. "It's hot out," I told him when I took my books back.

It was. Even though it was only April, the sun was

beating down and drying up the puddles from last night's rain. It usually doesn't get hot this early in western Washington. In fact, sometimes it isn't even hot in June.

"Yo, Bones," two guys yelled when we reached the junior high.

I shoved the sack of cookies at him. "You want the rest?"

"What for? They're yours, aren't they?" He split to join his friends.

I crossed over to the grade school and met Jill and Lindsi, who were standing on the parking strip eyeing the junior high guys. "That Paul would be real cute if he wasn't so skinny," Jill said.

"And if he'd get some jeans that weren't two inches too short," Lindsi added.

I didn't dare look back at Bones. He hated people talking about him. I just shrugged and asked the girls if they wanted some cookies. They dug into my sack together.

It wasn't until we were in the classroom, and Mrs. Shivelly was taking roll, that it dawned on me what I should have told Bones. I should have told him my pajamas got soaked in the rain. That would have proved I didn't dream the digging at midnight.

2

MRS. BORG had pulled the rocking chair smack in front of the TV. While her head craned forward to see a taxi follow a Corvette across the screen, her right foot rolled the wheel of Jimmy's buggy back and forth. I dumped my books and sweater on the couch and came over to see how he was doing.

His little mouth was pressed into a thin line and his round blue eyes were swimming with tears. "He stinks," I told Mrs. Borg.

"Shhh." She waved her hand at me.

"He smells," I said. "He's filled his pants."

Mrs. Borg kept shushing me. "Just a minute. Just a minute. This is almost over."

Mom came in the front door.

"Jimmy needs attention," I told her.

Mrs. Borg jumped out of the rocking chair. "Oh, Mrs. LeBlanc. I didn't expect you home so early. I was about to change the baby."

Sure.

"That's fine," Mom said. "Have you given him his bath?"

"No, I was going to do it just before you were due home so he'd be nice and fresh for you."

"That's fine," Mom said again. She'd sat down on the couch and was leaning back against the pillows.

"Aren't you going to say hello to Jimmy?" I asked her.

She turned her head to watch Mrs. Borg wheel him into the bathroom. "I think I'll wait until he's had his bath."

I gathered up my sweater and books and headed for the stairs.

"Wait a minute," Mom said. "I saw something that might interest you."

"What?"

"I saw a moving van parked in front of the house next to the Dormans'. A woman and girl about your age were carrying clothes up the steps."

"Maybe I'll check that out." I dumped the books

back on the couch. I didn't need to lug them a block and a half down the road.

Both the Dormans' house and the one beside it are made of whitewashed brick. They're nice enough, but the Dormans don't keep theirs up. The grass is always too long and the bushes grow above the windows. Mrs. Dorman is deaf, and I don't think she has much control over her sons. I remember my mom saying those boys needed a father to hold them in line. She thought it was terrible when they dropped out of high school four years ago.

They must be twenty by now. Or at least Bob is. I've never really talked to either Bob or Derek. They've got a mean bulldog in their backyard. Actually, nobody in the neighborhood knows much about them, except maybe Bones.

The movers came out of the house next to the Dormans'. I stood on my side of the street and watched them lug a flowered couch out of the van and up the steps. They stopped to shift the couch around before they hauled it onto the porch. A girl held the screen door open for them.

After the men were inside, she came down to get some more clothes from the green station wagon that was parked in front of the van. She was about my size, maybe a little chubbier, and had honey-colored hair that sprang from her head in kinky waves. My hair's lighter and shorter and the waves are looser. But she was wearing the kind of jeans my mom would never pay for.

The girl piled jackets and sweats over her arm, closed the car door, and stood looking over at me. "Hi," she said.

"Hi," I said back.

"You live around here?" She'd come almost to the curb on her side.

I moved to the curb on my side. "I live about a block and a half up the road."

"Any other kids in the neighborhood?"

"There's a boy next door to me. And one two blocks down from you. There's another girl up the street, but she goes to a Catholic school so she isn't around much."

"Do you go to Cascade Elementary?"

I nodded.

She hitched the load of clothes closer to her chest. "I'll probably see you at school tomorrow then. That's where my mom registered me."

"Probably." Or probably not. I was going to tell her there were eight sixth grade classes, but I didn't even know if she was in sixth grade. She went up the steps and I walked on home.

The next morning, I met Bones in front of his house. I was eating an apple and held out another one for him. He hesitated a second before taking it. By the frown that crossed his forehead, I could tell he didn't like me giving him things, but it was that or let him starve to death.

"Find out who's digging up your yard?" I asked.

"No."

"It was raining when I watched that person dig the other night and my pajamas got wet."

Bones just lifted one eyebrow. So much for that topic.

"The babysitter we have spends all her time watching TV," I said after I'd chomped up most of my apple.

"Fire her."

"I can't, and Mom won't believe Jimmy has a diaper rash because Mrs. Borg is too lazy to change him. She never feeds him either."

"What?!"

That got me too much attention. I backed off from Bones's stare. "Well, she feeds him, but only when her soap opera's over."

Bones turned away from me to toss his apple core into the gutter.

"Hi!" the new girl called from her yard. "Are you guys going to school?"

"Ya," I called back.

She zipped across the street. "Hi, I'm Melissa, but everybody calls me Missy."

"I'm Caitlin. And that's Paul, but everybody calls him—"

Bones had looked Missy over, decided she didn't

13

interest him, and was halfway down the block. I shrugged my shoulders. "I call him Bones."

"Friendly guy."

"Short attention span."

Missy giggled. "You said you went to Cascade."

"I do," I told her.

"But isn't it on my side of the street?"

"Yes, but the junior high is on this side and that's where Bones goes to school."

"Oh."

As we walked, Missy took in the houses and yards and flowering trees. I scuffed along beside her feeling my stomach sink with disappointment. She'd probably expect me to go to school with her every morning and I'd get cheated out of walking with Bones. I figured she was the gabby kind of girl who Bones wouldn't hold still for.

"What does your dad do?" Missy asked.

"He goes around the country teaching people how to be long-term-care insurance agents. That's what my mom is. What do your folks do?"

"My dad's a hypnotist and my mom works in his office."

"I never heard of a hypnotist having an office."

"The entertainment kind don't, but my dad does clinical hypnosis. You know, like curing people who are fat or smoke. Let's cross here, okay?"

We crossed over and immediately ran into Arthur

14

who was coming down the path from his house. I introduced him to Missy. "Her dad's a hypnotist," I told him.

Arthur snaked his hands in front of Missy's face. "You are getting sleepier and sleepier."

"That's old," Missy said.

Jill and Lindsi were hanging out near the entrance to Cascade. Robert was with them. "How come you didn't walk with Paul?" Jill asked me.

"Because I came with Missy. This is Missy."

Everyone said, "Hi, hi," and then Lindsi noticed Arthur had on Reeboks. "How come?" she asked. Arthur usually wore brown leather shoes.

"I got them for my birthday," Arthur said. "I got a new computer, too. A 486."

"I got a new plane for my birthday," Robert said. "A 747."

Everyone laughed but Arthur.

Lindsi took a look at the registration paper Missy was holding. "Too bad you have Jenkins," Lindsi said.

"Is he a jerk?" Missy asked.

"Not exactly a jerk, but it'd be better if you had Snivelly with us," Robert said.

Missy wrinkled her face. "Snivelly?"

The warning bell rang and four of us went into Mrs. Shivelly's room while Missy went down the hall to Jenkins.

MRS. BORG had managed to give Jimmy a bath before I got home. After I'd filled myself up with raspberry juice and cookies, I took him out to the backyard. He lay on his blanket and watched the apple blossoms flutter, while I peeked through the fence at the Reddings' yard. I couldn't see a fresh mound of dirt anywhere. I did see Bones come out of his toolshed. I pulled my head back fast and sat down on the edge of Jimmy's blanket to think.

How could I find out what Bones was doing without alarming him? The swing. The swing! Jimmy loved to swing.

He gurgled in my lap while we swung higher and higher. By clutching Jimmy with one hand and holding the rope with the other, I was able to catch glimpses of the Reddings' whole backyard. All Bones was doing was weeding the vegetable garden. He wasn't even near the place where I'd seen someone digging.

Mrs. Kager was. She was on the other side of the fence, clipping at her rose bushes and keeping an eye on Bones. She's a nosy old thing. The Kagers have an ancient house and a huge yard that goes along the back of ours and the Reddings'. Mr. Kager's lost most of his marbles and Mrs. Kager has to hold his hand when they walk to the store.

I slowed down the swing, thinking I might take Jimmy over to visit Bones. But when I got a look at Jimmy's bloodless lips, I realized the spring breeze was too much for him. He had just a cotton shirt and pants on over his diapers. I put him down on his blanket and ran inside for the snowsuit Mom had saved from when I was a baby.

Jimmy waves his arms and kicks his legs to avoid being trapped in the suit. My patience was gone by the time I got him stuffed inside. I sat him up with his back toward me and pulled up the zipper.

He let out a scream. I turned him around and held him in the air. The snowsuit was on. His arms and legs were fine. Still he screamed. "Jimmy," I said, "I'm only trying to keep you warm."

Tears were running down his little face, which had turned bright red. "Jimmy, come on. You can't catch cold out here."

He screamed even louder.

Bones came through the side gate. "What are you doing to that kid?"

"Nothing," I told him. "I don't think he likes to wear the snowsuit."

Bones kneeled down beside me. "When did you put it on him?"

"Just before he started yelling."

"Give him to me." Bones took Jimmy in his lap and peeled down the zipper. It stuck where Jimmy's tummy bulged out from his shirt. "Way to go. You zipped in his skin."

"Oh, no." I cringed while Bones eased Jimmy's flesh out of the zipper.

Jimmy's screams gradually turned to sobs, then hiccups, as Bones rubbed the welt the zipper had left on his tummy.

"That's better, huh kid?" Bones said to Jimmy. Jimmy stared fascinated up into Bones's gray eyes.

"Here, you can have him now." Bones handed the baby to me. "You better take him inside."

I hugged Jimmy to my chest and watched Bones go back through the gate and into his own yard.

3

JUST as I thought, I got stuck walking to school with Missy. I started out with Bones the next day, but when Missy called hi from her side of the street, Bones said, "You better go over there with your new friend."

What else could I do? And just as I thought, she was a gabby girl. She told me she was adopted, that her real mother was seventeen when she'd had her, and her adoptive mother sent her real mother to college in exchange for Missy.

I tried to top this by telling her about my French ancestors who'd escaped the guillotine by fleeing to

19

Quebec. It was one of my dad's favorite stories. Missy was impressed.

"That's why you have the French name, LeBlanc," she said.

We'd come up to Arthur's house by then and I didn't want to be caught bragging in front of him, so I changed the subject to hypnosis. "Have you ever been hypnotized?" I asked Missy.

"Sure, lots of times."

Arthur had pulled in behind us and he asked, "Who does it? Your dad?"

"Ya," Missy said. "He puts me under so deep, I don't even feel it when he sticks a needle through my hand."

Weird, I thought.

Arthur didn't believe it. "Come on now. You don't feel *anything?*" He had his nose poked right between Missy and me as he trotted to keep up.

"What else does your dad do with you?" I wanted to know.

"Well, he taught me about hypnogogic times. You can use that when you want to predict things."

"What things?" I asked.

"Say you want to know what your teacher will wear the next day. After you go to bed at night, and as soon as you feel yourself falling asleep, you think of your teacher standing in front of the room. Then you can see what she'll be wearing."

20

"Woo woo." Arthur wiggled his arms at the blue sky.

"You're walking on my heels," I snapped. Arthur pulled his arms in.

"I'll try it on Snivelly," I decided. "Now, how exactly do you do it?"

"Just before you fall asleep," Missy said patiently, "when things in your head begin to get swimmy, you picture what you want to see. Or you can do it just as you're coming out of a dream in the morning, before you open your eyes or hear your mom call you. My dad teaches his patients that those are suggestible times and has them tell themselves that they'll eat vegetables all day."

"Come to me, broccoli," Arthur sang out. "I'm hypnogagging."

"Shut up, Arthur. Listen, Missy, I'll try it on my teacher when my baby brother cries tonight. That's when I'm real groggy. And you try it on Mr. Jenkins. I want to see if this works."

"It works," Missy said.

That night, as soon as Jimmy's whimpers brought me up from sleep, I told myself I'd see Mrs. Shivelly. But I didn't exactly see her. It wasn't like a snapshot. Instead, I got the impression she was dropping something small on one of our desks. I thought she had more of the things in a box.

When Jimmy's whimpers turned to yowls, I realized nothing I'd seen had been in color. Rats. And I really

21

didn't even know if Mrs. Shivelly was wearing a skirt or a dress.

In the morning, I left Bones at the end of our block and crossed over to Missy's side. She was waiting on the sidewalk at the bottom of her steps. "What's Jenkins going to wear today?" I asked her.

"Brown," she said.

"He had on a brown suit yesterday."

"I can't help it. That's what he's going to wear today."

Hmmm, I didn't know about this. "All I saw was Snivelly passing out something. But I didn't see any colors."

Missy shrugged. "Maybe you don't see colors. Do you dream in color?"

"I don't know. I don't remember."

She slung her book bag over to her other shoulder. She *was* kinda plump. She wore cute clothes, though. I guess you can if you're an only child. I usually wore Levis and T-shirts. I made sure my shirts had *Esprit* on them or something like that. If you're careful, you can blend right in. The reason kids noticed Bones's clothes was because Mrs. Redding hadn't bought him any new jeans for a year.

"You know," Missy said, "there's something weird about those Dormans. They're always knocking each other around and they come in and out all night.

22

There's something going on in that shed behind their house, too."

"What?"

"I don't know, but I'd sure like to find out."

Good luck with the bulldog, I wanted to say, but I wasn't sure if I liked Missy or not.

When I got into class I saw that Mrs. Shivelly was wearing a blue dress and that she had all our morning assignments on the blackboard. Kids like Arthur are interested in knowing what they have to do, but it just depresses me. Arthur can get all his work done in two hours and then spend the rest of the time before lunch playing on the computers in the back of the room.

Before Mrs. Shivelly had the roll called, Arthur had his math book out and was zooming through a page of division problems. Watching him zip all those little decimals around made me sick. I pulled out my spelling book. Since that was the shortest assignment, I did it first.

The only advantage of having to share a table with Arthur is that I get to use his space when he goes back to the computers. He insists that I keep all my stuff on my side when he's sitting with me. He even has red tape dividing our table in half. Mrs. Shivelly let him do it. She thinks he's organized. I think he's obnoxious.

At ten-fifteen, he smacked his history book closed. "Well, I'm finished."

Mrs. Shivelly looked up from helping Lindsi with her decimals. She didn't even chew him out for disturbing the class.

Jill sits at the table in front of me. When she got up to go to the library, I checked the clock. Only thirty-five minutes until lunch. I hurried through the rest of the assignments so I wouldn't have to lug my books home.

I eat lunch over at Lindsi's desk. She has one of the few single places in the room. Jill always joins us. Robert usually turns his chair halfway around so he can talk to us while he's eating. Arthur sits by himself. Nobody wants to spend their lunchtime listening to what a big brain he is.

We played volleyball during lunch recess. Missy and some girls from her class played against us. "Mr. Jenkins has on his brown suit," she called over to me.

Lindsi had the ball poised in one hand, getting ready to serve. "So what? Jenkins either wears a brown suit or a gray suit." She bammed the ball to the lefthand corner and Missy bammed it back.

There was a long line at the drinking fountain when we got in from lunch recess. I waited for a turn anyway because I was sweaty and thirsty. By the time I got in the classroom, most of the kids were sitting down, staring at gray lumps on their desks. "What're these things?" I asked Arthur.

Arthur was poking his lump with the end of his pencil. "I don't know yet."

I took my pencil out and rolled my lump over.

"It's dead," Jill said.

"Ya, I'm making sure," Robert said and cut his in half.

Mrs. Shively was standing in front of the room with a smile on her face. It was science time and she gets happy making us curious. "Take out a piece of paper," she said, "and write down your observations. Use your sense of smell and feel. You probably don't want to use your sense of taste."

"Mine has claws," Aaron said.

"Mine's crunchy," Robert said.

"What makes you think that?" Mrs. Shively asked him.

"I cut it and it crunched."

Stephanie held her lump away from her nose by pinching it with her scissors. "Totally gross!"

"What makes you think it's gross?" Mrs. Shively asked.

"Smells bad," Stephanie said.

"Like dirt," Jaime added.

"Mine seems hairy," Jill said.

"An observation is something that you see. Not

25

something you know," Mrs. Shivelly told us. "If you're not sure, write down that it *appears* to be hairy."

I wrote down that mine appeared to be hairy. I could see that Arthur had written, *1 ½" long, gray-black, bony, fur.* I added those things, too.

"There's some white stuff in mine." By now, Robert had his lump cut into little pieces. "It looks like doo-doo."

"Those are bones," Arthur told him.

"Why do you think they're bones?" Mrs. Shivelly asked.

"Because I can see joints in a leg."

Mrs. Shivelly's smile grew wider. Arthur was obviously on the right track.

"I'm going to pass out some dental tools to help you dissect what you have," Mrs. Shivelly told us. "Don't lose any of the parts. I'm also going to give you each a sheet of black paper to keep them on. When you think you know the name of what you have, write it below your observations."

I poked my lump apart with the silver dental tool. Wound up in the furry hair, I found something that looked like a tiny horse's skull. "Is this a skull?" I asked Arthur.

He looked over at the stuff on my black paper. "What do you think?"

"If I knew, I wouldn't ask you, stupid," I said. Arthur gets prissy when he wants to beat everyone else at figuring something out. I waited until he was concentrating on taking the last bit of his lump apart before I shot a glance at his observation sheet. At the bottom he'd written *owl pellet.*

Owl pellet? Whatever. I wrote that down. But when Mrs. Shivelly asked the class how many students knew what they had, I didn't raise my hand. Arthur did.

So did Aaron. Mrs. Shivelly called on him. "Animal droppings," he said.

Mrs. Shivelly tilted her head to the side. "Close, but not quite. Arthur?"

"Owl pellet."

She beamed at him. "Exactly. And this particular owl pellet came out of the owl's mouth. One thing an owl eats is a vole. Its body digests the meat and it regurgitates the vole's fur and bones.

"Owls don't have teeth. They swallow gravel to help grind their food. There's dirt in the gravel and the vole has dirt on it, so your pellets smell like dirt. The owl may eat several voles before it regurgitates. Your pellets may have more than one skeleton. What I want you to do is put one vole skeleton together on your black paper. I'll hand out a packet that will list the bones you need and show you how a vole's skeleton should look.

"Some of you may have two skulls or no skull or

one femur or three femurs. You may trade parts with each other if you wish."

Mrs. Shivelly passed out the packets and we got to work. My tiny horse's skull was a vole's skull all right. I found two iliums and three mandibles and a bunch of little vertebrae. Mrs. Shivelly said vertebrae would be easy to identify because they had holes where the spinal cord had gone through.

I poked and poked through my pellet, but I couldn't find more than one scapula. "I'll trade you a mandible for a scapula," I told Arthur.

He didn't even answer me. Jill turned around. "I'll trade you."

Good. Now I had to find the rib bones. I'd found three when Robert leaned across to Arthur who was crouched over his black paper. "You've got two skulls. How about trading me for something?"

"No," Arthur said. "You probably had a skull, but cut it to pieces."

"You're such a jerk, Arthur," I said.

Arthur straightened up to give me an indignant stare. "He probably did cut it."

I stared right back at him. "So?"

Tracy hadn't been in class for the morning roll call. She came in the room now and gave Mrs. Shivelly her excuse. Mrs. Shivelly explained what we were doing before she went to her desk and got a dental tool, paper, packet, and owl pellet for Tracy. It was when

Mrs. Shivelly took the pellet out of a box that it hit me.

The hypnogogic time! I had seen her take something small out of a box and drop it on a desk. I hadn't seen any kids in the room. Of course I hadn't, because Mrs. Shivelly had done this while we were out at lunch recess.

Chills crawled up my arms as I realized Missy's directions had really worked. I wondered what else she'd told the truth about. Did her dad actually stick needles through her hand?

4

DAD was sitting in the rocker holding Jimmy when I got home. "How's school?" he asked me.

"The usual." I gave him a big kiss and hug. "And how was Florida or whatever?"

"It was Chicago and the usual. Dull hotel room and windy weather."

I looked down at Jimmy sleeping in Dad's arms. "Isn't he cute?"

"Mrs. Borg had him on the floor on a blanket when I got here. He managed to hitch himself forward a couple inches."

"He did! We better not put him to bed in his buggy anymore."

Dad traced Jimmy's downy eyebrow with his finger. "Yep, I think we'll have to take him upstairs to the crib."

Mom agreed with this when she came home. While she got dinner, Dad and I made up Jimmy's bed in the room next to mine. "I wish we had a bottle warmer and a small refrigerator up here," I told Dad. "Then I wouldn't have to go downstairs for his bottle in the middle of the night."

"Well, it won't be too long until he's sleeping through." Dad ruffled my hair before he took one end of the blue quilt from me. "You're a sweetheart, Caitlin."

Things cheer up in our house when Dad's home. And Mom makes better meals. We had broiled salmon, brown rice, artichokes, and a salad made out of curly lettuce and strawberries. "What's for dessert?" I asked.

"Häagen-Dazs," Mom said. "Swiss Almond. You can serve it."

While we ate our ice cream, Mom complained to Dad about the number of people who'd canceled their insurance policies. "I felt like I'd been doing volunteer work when I picked up my check last Monday."

"Well, you have to figure the percentages," Dad told

her. "The more appointments you have, the more chances you have for good sales."

Mom frowned into her coffee cup. "It also depends on the number of leads the company gives me each week."

"Yes, leads are down this month," he said. "That's why you need to build up your referrals."

My sister Susan came over after dinner. She's a salesperson for Dad's company, too. When she started complaining about her lack of leads, I went up to my room to read a book. I can only stand so much insurance talk.

I was reading *Captives of Time.* It's a story about a girl in the fourteenth century who sees her parents murdered by soldiers and escapes with her younger brother who can't talk. I got so involved in the book, I was still awake when my sister left.

Mom came up to check on Jimmy and found my light on. "Caitlin! It's after eleven. Get in bed and get to sleep. You have to go to school tomorrow."

It seemed like I had just closed my eyes when I was awakened by a scraping shovel again. I'm a very light sleeper and any strange noise in the house will wake me up. Because I sleep with my window open, anything strange next door will wake me up, too.

At first I thought, I'll just go back to sleep. It's none of my business.

But I didn't. I became more and more curious and more and more wide awake. Finally, I threw off my covers, put on my bathrobe and slippers, and padded over to the French doors to ease them open.

It wasn't raining, but there was no moon to light the yard. I crouched down and waddled to the end of the deck. By peering through the railing, I could barely make out a figure by the white fence. It was moving. And it was moving in time to the sound of a shovel.

If I waited until the digging was finished, I thought, I would see the person walk. That way, I could tell if it was Bones.

I'd been sitting on the deck just a few minues, when I heard a door creak open. The only one that creaks is the Reddings' basement door. It's on the side of their house facing ours. I scooted myself back toward my room and looked down through the side railing. Someone else was slowly inching toward the backyard.

What I did next was dumb. It seemed smart when I first thought of it. I thought, I'll go inside my room and turn on my light. The light will reflect on the Reddings' house. And, if I lean out my window, I can see who's doing the creeping.

That's what I did. But the light in my room blinded me from seeing into the dark. All I caught was a shadow moving swiftly back to the basement door. When the door creaked again, I knew I'd blown it.

I listened a while to see if the digging would continue. But there was only the sound of a car going down the street. I gave up and went to bed, but not to sleep. I kept thinking and thinking that one of the two people out there had to be Bones, but which? I was still trying to figure that out when Jimmy howled for his bottle.

In the morning, I was too sleepy to pack up any food for Bones. While I listened for the slam of his back door, I tried to plan what I'd say. Something casual that might get him talking, but wouldn't make him turn on me for spying.

I met him on the sidewalk in front of his house. "Lots of action at your place in the middle of the night, huh?" I said.

Bones didn't answer me. He has long eyelashes. When he narrows his eyes and stares straight ahead, his black lashes look like half-closed butterfly wings. I walked beside him saying nothing more. He said nothing. If he knew what was going on in the night, he wasn't about to tell me.

His mother was in our kitchen having coffee with my mom when I got home from school. Mrs. Redding has salt-and-pepper hair that she rolls into a bun at the back of her neck. Once her hair must have been all black like Bones's is. Last summer, I saw her pulling dandelions in her front yard. A breeze had loosened her hair, making her look almost pretty.

She wasn't pretty this afternoon. Her face was draggy with discontent. "This is the second time the assessor has raised the taxes in the last five years."

"Well," Mom said, "that means our property value has gone up."

"But it doesn't do me any good. I couldn't afford to move."

"You have three bedrooms," Mom told her. "Why don't you get a roomer?"

"And let them wreck the whole house?"

"Get a quiet old lady." Mom smiled at me while I got a bottle of grape juice out of the refrigerator and poured myself a drink.

Mrs. Redding was too busy pitying herself to notice. "The last thing I need is another old lady snooping around in my business. Mrs. Kager is bad enough."

So, Mrs. Redding doesn't like anyone snooping around, I thought. Hmmm.

Mom picked up her coffee cup and took it to the sink. "I'd better get on the phone and make some more appointments. Two canceled on me today."

"Two!" I was leaning against the refrigerator drinking my grape juice. "How much are you going to make this week?"

35

"Not much," Mom said.

Mrs. Redding looked up at her. "At least you have a husband to support you."

"And a new baby and doctor bills." Mom took the cream pitcher off the kitchen table, another obvious signal that coffee time was over. I moved aside to let her put it in the fridge. Mrs. Redding didn't budge.

"Don't you have health care benefits?" she asked Mom.

"No, we're independent agents."

I could see that Mrs. Redding didn't know how to top this with more misery of her own. She slowly got up from the table. "Those are pretty earrings, Caitlin. I wish I could buy Paul extra things."

Like food, I thought to myself.

"My sister sent them for Caitlin's birthday." Mom opened the kitchen door. "Thanks for spending part of your day off with me, Edith."

"I'm glad I caught you home. I can't go to the mall and spend money."

Mom closed the door firmly after Mrs. Redding started down the steps. "That woman is so depressing."

"How come she's so poor?" I asked. "She's got a steady job being a receptionist at the nursing home. Does she have a lot of bills or something?"

"I doubt it. Her mortgage was paid off when Tom Redding died," Mom said. "She just thinks poor."

"She acts poor, too. She feeds Bones blue milk."

"Blue milk?"

"Ya, blue milk. I was over there helping Bones pick apples off their tree last fall. When we finished, she invited me in for a snack. I thought I was going to get something good and I wondered why Bones told her we were full from eating apples.

"Mrs. Redding said to come in and have some cookies anyway. So I went in and Bones lagged behind me. I figured out why when she brought out the cookies. They were hard homemade things that tasted like flour. There weren't any chocolate chips or raisins in them or anything."

While I was telling this to Mom, I was putting the teaspoons in the dishwasher. It's my job to keep the kitchen clean.

"What's this about blue milk?" Mom asked.

"That's what she gave us to go with the cookies. Real thin milk. Not just two percent, but bluer. Bones went back outside before I finished getting down my cookies. When I was leaving the kitchen, I saw her put the carton of milk under the sink faucet. I thought she was going to wash it out. But she wasn't. She let some water run in it and then put the carton back in the refrigerator. Can you believe it?"

Mom shook her head. "That woman's gotten more and more neurotic since her husband died."

"Ya, but what about Bones? He's getting skinnier and skinnier."

"Oh, he'll survive. Boys are tough." Mom had her box of insurance leads and was moving toward the wall phone. I might have told her about the midnight digging then, but I could see her mind wasn't on the Reddings anymore.

5

IT wasn't until Sunday night that I heard the digging again. I didn't feel curious this time. I just wanted some sleep. Jimmy had a cold and he'd whimpered me awake twice before twelve o'clock.

He wasn't really hungry. He took about three sips from the bottle and then spit out the nipple. What he wanted was cuddling.

The second time he'd gotten up, I almost rocked myself to sleep before his eyes closed. I was barely back in bed when the scraping of a shovel began. It was worse than a faucet dripping. I wanted to go to my window, shout, "Shut up out there," and slam down the window.

The longer the digging went on, the madder I got. Whoever was doing it must be trying for China. I turned over to look at my night clock. The hands pointed to one-twenty. That did it.

I got out of bed and marched to my French doors. I was about to yank them open, when a cooler thought swirled into my brain. Now take it easy, Caitlin, I said to myself. Creep out there and stay there this time until you know who it is.

And that's what I did. It was the first of May and the stars were shining, giving a slight gleam to the night. In the same spot, in the exact same spot over by the white fence, the person was digging.

When I'd swung Jimmy up to look at Bones weeding his garden, I hadn't seen a pile of dirt by this fence. The ground didn't look disturbed. This is where Mrs. Redding grew her dahlias and it was too early in the year for their sprouts to show.

It was also too early to be warm at night. The cold sent shivers along my body as I sat by the deck railing peering down at the person digging. It looked like Bones this time. The movements were like Bones's. Fast and coordinated.

But of course I wasn't positive. Forget the cold, I told myself, you're staying here until the digging's done and you see the person walk. I wrapped my arms around my shoulders and waited. And waited.

The shadowy figure crouched down. And stayed down. I poked my forehead against the railing, but it was too dark to see what was going on over there. Something. There was a faint clinking sound. Then nothing. Then it seemed as if the figure was flat on the ground. Maybe putting something in a hole. Or getting something out. Or putting something back. Or?

The shadow stretched up. There were little movements, maybe hands and arms, but not enough for me to be certain. Then the figure bent over. It was to pick up the shovel, because after that I heard scraping sounds and saw arms swing back and forth.

The hole was getting filled up, I was sure. And even surer when the figure crouched again and seemed to be smoothing the earth. I watched carefully as the shadow rose and moved toward the shed. This is it, I thought, but the dark of the night swallowed the figure in seconds.

That's all right, I told myself, if it's Bones, I'll see him when he goes in his back door. I scooted over to the side rail and strained my eyes searching for a glimpse of him. Once I thought I heard a door close, but it could have been a branch breaking.

A light came on in the Kager house and then went

off. My legs got stiff from crouching on the hard deck and I finally gave up. Who cares? I thought. I'm freezing.

When I was back in bed, still shivering under my covers, I realized Bones could have gone around to his front door. And he would have if he thought I might be watching. Anyway, I wasn't going to ask him about the digging. He wouldn't tell me anything if I did.

I told Missy about it, though. And then felt guilty for betraying Bones. She had invited me into her house on the way home from school.

"I'll have to call the babysitter first," I said.

She offered to let me use her phone, so we went on up her stairs.

It took seven rings to tear Mrs. Borg away from the TV. I wanted to tell her to turn it off and pay attention to Jimmy because he was sick. But all I told her was that I'd be home in an hour.

Missy and I sat on stools at the breakfast bar and drank Cokes and ate brownies. "What kind of frosting is this?" I asked.

"German chocolate." Missy licked some off her fingers. "Mom gets these at Olson's. Good, aren't they?"

I nodded and helped myself to a second one. Missy took her third. It was easy to see why she was chubby.

"Listen," Missy said, "how well do you know the Dormans?"

"Not very well. I've heard my mom and Mrs. Redding talking about them when they've gotten in trouble with the police."

"Well." Missy leaned an elbow on the marble bar and widened her pale blue eyes. "Something fishy is going on over there. They've got this bulldog in the backyard. He can run around inside the fence when the guys are gone, but when they're home, they chain him up. I think they do that so he doesn't scare the people that visit them."

"I've never seen anybody visit them."

Missy wiped her mouth with a paper napkin before taking her fourth brownie. That left one on the plate. I was full, but they tasted so yummy I couldn't see leaving it for her. I picked it up, held it in the air, and stuck out my tongue to lick the sides where the golden frosting lapped over. If I hadn't been a guest, I would have licked the frosting off the top, too, and then put the brownie back on the plate. But since this was my first visit, I crammed down the whole thing while Missy went on about the Dormans.

"The reason you don't see the visitors," she explained, "is that they come in the alleyway. They come at night, too. And I think they're all guys because when Dad heard one of their cars roar up the alley, he said it was against the law to have mufflers that loud.

"Anyway." Missy opened her eyes even wider. "I've looked out the bathroom window when I've gotten up to go in the night. Every time a car drives up, one of the Dorman brothers comes out, chains the dog, and opens the toolshed in the backyard. I know they do that because they turn on a light in there."

"What's in the shed?"

Missy wiped both her hands and mouth this time and pushed the plate to the back of the bar. "That's the part I don't know. But listen. If we made friends with that dog, we could find out."

A picture of the bulldog's huge jaws, studded with sharp teeth, flashed in my head. "I don't know about that."

"He just looks mean. I've seen him paw Derek to get petted."

"Sounds risky to me. And even if we did make friends with him, how're we going to find out what's in the shed?"

"Simple. Simple. We climb over the fence."

The next picture in my head was of the white bulldog standing on his bowlegged hind legs, ripping at the bottom of my jeans while I tried to scramble back over the fence. "I don't know, Missy."

She jumped down from her stool. "Come on. It might take a couple days to get him to trust us. Let's start now."

I stayed on my stool and watched her open the refrigerator door. She pulled out a beef roast, put it on the counter, took a knife out of the drawer, and hacked three chunks off the roast. I'd never dare to do that when my mom wasn't home.

She pulled the plastic wrap over the roast and put it back in the fridge. I slipped from my stool and followed her out the kitchen door. The bulldog was sleeping under a tree in the Dormans' yard. His flabby jowls hung down in the grass while snorts blew out of his smashed-in nose.

Missy kneeled by the wire fence. "Here, Wigger. Here, Wigger."

"Wigger?" I said.

"That's what I heard them call him." She poked a piece of meat through the wire. "Come on, boy. Here, Wigger."

Wigger opened one round eye.

"Wigger, come on. Meat, boy. Come and get it."

"He's not going to move his fat self," I told Missy.

She stood up and tossed the piece of meat over the fence. Wigger watched it fall about ten feet away from him. He slowly heaved himself onto his bowlegs, waddled over to the meat, and gave it a couple of sniffs. Then he stopped to eye us suspiciously before he downed it in one gulp.

"See, that was good," Missy told him. "Here's some more. See? See? Come and get it. Come on, Wigger."

Wigger stared at the second piece of meat Missy poked through the wire. He didn't move, though. She threw the meat over the fence so it landed halfway between us and him. He inched forward to where the meat had fallen and gulped it down.

"Good boy," Missy praised him. "You're a good boy. Now come and get this one."

No way. Wigger wouldn't budge. Missy tossed the last piece so it dropped about two feet from us. Wigger hung his head a long time before he inched forward again, grabbed the meat, and went back to lie down under his tree, keeping his beady eyes on us.

"He doesn't look too friendly to me," I said.

"That's okay," she said. "It'll take a while. In my other house, I got a chipmunk to come into the kitchen for nuts."

I was thinking that Wigger wasn't any chipmunk, as I followed Missy back in the house. But I didn't want to say too much. Missy just might make friends with him.

"What's your Mom going to say about her roast being hacked up?" I asked when we were in the living room.

Missy flopped down on the flowered couch. "I'll tell her I fried up the meat to make sandwiches for my guest."

"Three sandwiches and seven brownies?"

"Well, guests then. What's that skinny guy that lives next door to you like?"

"He's sort of quiet, but he's real kind to animals and babies." Something inside me knew I shouldn't say any more, but I did. "There's funny goings on at his place, too."

"What?"

"Somebody digs a hole in their backyard at night and covers it up so it doesn't show in the daytime."

"Do you see them?" Missy was giving me her complete attention. She obviously loved gossip.

"A little bit in the dark. They woke me up digging last night. This morning I looked out from my deck, but there was no hole in their yard."

"Hmmm. He looks poor. Maybe he's burying garbage so they don't have to pay the garbage man."

That couldn't be it because I'd seen a second person sneaking around. I was feeling too guilty to tell her that, though. Bones has always been nice to Jimmy and me. "I'd better be going. I told the babysitter I'd be home in an hour."

Missy walked to her door with me. "Come on over tomorrow," she said, "and we'll feed Wigger some more."

6

THE junior high starts ten minutes before the elementary school does and gets out ten minutes earlier. Since Missy'd moved in, I'd given up hurrying out of my classroom and running to catch up with Bones. Missy always waited for me in the school hallway. Her room was closer to the outside doors than mine.

"You're coming to my house to work on Wigger, aren't you?" she asked as soon as I joined her.

"I guess so," I said. "But I can't stay long. I have to learn the names of the arteries in the body. We're having a health test tomorrow."

"We're still putting our voles together," she said. "Jenkins is so boringly slow."

Arthur was walking in front of us. He shoved the door open by pushing on the bar with his books. I grabbed the bar from behind him before the door shut on us. He couldn't hold it open, of course. He's such an irritating little jerk.

Missy and I gossiped about teachers all the way to her house. I thought Mrs. Shivelly knew more about science than Mr. Jenkins did. Missy agreed. "But Jenkins can umpire better than Snively can. She doesn't even know a tie goes to the runner."

And I had to agree about that.

Ahead of us, I could see Bob Dorman leaning on his car talking to someone. Just as we started up Missy's steps, I turned to take a second look. Bones! The person beside Bob was Bones. He flicked a glance up the stairs before he went on with his conversation. It gave me a sinking feeling in my stomach to see him hang out with a Dorman.

When we got in Missy's house, we looked out her bathroom window. Derek was in his backyard, whirling around in a circle with a rag flying from one hand. Wigger was leaping in the air, trying to grab the rag.

"You wouldn't think that fat dog could jump so high," I said after Missy closed the window.

"We can't feed him now with those guys around.

What do you want to do? Shall we make some popcorn?"

We made popcorn and sat at her breakfast bar munching it. Missy's birthday was coming up in a week and she was hoping her mom would let her have a party. "I might be able to get Dad to hypnotize me. Do you think the kids would like that?"

"If he put a needle through your hand," I said.

Bones wasn't around when I left Missy's house. I'd been so preoccupied thinking about him talking to Bob Dorman that I'd forgotten to call Mrs. Borg. Mom was home when I got there and she was mad.

As soon as she put the phone down, she turned on me. "Caitlin, just where have you been? It doesn't take you an hour to walk home from school."

"I know," I said. "I stopped at Missy's for a while."

"The rule around here is that you come directly home or call to tell us where you are."

"I know, but—"

Mom flapped her appointment book in my face. "I don't want to hear any 'buts.' Go get the clippers and trim the grass under the apple tree. Make yourself useful for a change."

Useful? I got up in the night with Jimmy. I cleaned the kitchen. I baby-sat when she wanted to do her book-work.

I didn't tell her all this. She was obviously in a bad mood. Her afternoon appointments probably canceled. I put on my oldest jeans, got the clippers, and went out to the backyard, mumbling to myself.

My mumbling turned to swearing in about ten minutes. The clippers kept sticking. Instead of springing wide like they were supposed to after every cut, they stayed closed and I had to pull the blades apart before I could cut again. About the twenty-fifth time I pried them open, I yelled out a four-letter word and threw the clippers across the yard. They hit the fence with a whack.

Bones came through the gate. "What's going on?"

"Those stupid clippers keep sticking." I was sitting under the tree gnawing at my knuckles.

Bones went over to the edge of the fence, picked up the clippers, and squeezed them a couple of times. "They need oiling."

He headed into his yard, so I followed him through the gate. While he oiled the clippers in his toolshed, I took a good look at the dahlia bed by his back fence. The bare ground was flat as a pancake.

"Here," he said, coming out of the toolshed. "Try them now."

I took the clippers and gave them a squeeze. They worked. "I saw you talking to Bob Dorman," I told Bones. "Do you like him?"

"He's nobody you want to know. Try the clippers on the grass."

"If you can know him, why can't I know him?"

"That's different. Don't you want to see if they cut?"

I bent down and gave his grass three snips. The clippers sprung open each time. "Perfect," I said. "Thanks."

He nodded and went back to the shed. I guessed he was going for his weeding tools so he could work in the garden. I could see his pea plants were already three inches high. At least he got to eat vegetables.

It took about a half hour to cut the long grass away from the tree trunk. When I was finished, I stood up and brushed the clippings off my jeans. "Say, girl! Say, girl!" Mr. Kager called. "Come here a minute."

I went over to the fence that separated our yards. "What do you want?"

"Say, girl, are you rich like that lady?" He pointed a bony finger at the Reddings' house.

"That woman's not rich," I told him.

"Oh, yes, she is. My wife seen her buying gold. Are you rich, too?"

"No, I'm not rich."

His finger wavered over to the house on the other side of the Reddings'. It's a three-story place that sticks up in the sky.

"See that house there," the old man said. The brown spotted skin on his face hung from his skull and I hated to look at him.

"See that house," he repeated. "I flew over that house this morning."

"Umm, that's nice," I said and turned away.

I tried to walk slowly across my yard while I felt his milky eyes follow me. In the living room, I said to Mom, "Everybody in our neighborhood's crazy. Old Mr. Kager thinks Mrs. Redding's rich and he said he flew over a house this morning."

"Maybe he's getting Alzheimer's," Mom said. "He's already got a bad heart. I couldn't insure him."

"Business, always business," I muttered and went upstairs to read.

MISSY was hopping up and down when I met her on the way to school the next morning. "Guess what?" she said.

"What?"

"I get to have a party and my dad will come and hypnotize me."

"Will he put a needle through your hand?"

"Oh, sure. He always does that."

"All the time?"

She frowned and pulled her head back as if I were stupid. "No, not all the time. Only at my parties."

Arthur came down his steps just as we got to his house. "Missy's going to have a party and her dad's going to shove a needle through her hand," I told him.

Arthur moved next to Missy and looked up into her face. "Is this for real?"

"Sure," she said. "Do you want to come?"

"Is it going to be mostly girls?"

"I don't know," Missy said. "It depends on who wants to come."

"Ask Robert," Arthur said.

Robert and Lindsi and Jill were standing out in front of the school when we got there. Missy invited all of them to her party. "It's a week from Friday," she told us. "Be there by five because we're having dinner. Pizza."

Pizza sounded good then, but by noon the thought of eating anything made me cringe. My throat hurt. It felt thick and sore and when I stood in line for lunch, all I wanted was some milk. After one swallow, I pushed even that away.

Mrs. Shively stopped by my desk with her lunch tray in one hand. "Caitlin, you're not eating."

"No," I whispered. "I think I've got my baby brother's cold."

"You sound like you have. You'd better run on down to the nurse and have her look at you."

I had to wait in the office until the nurse came back from her lunch. She pushed my tongue down with a stick, told me to say "ah," and shook her head over what she saw. "My, that's an angry-looking throat. We better call your mother and have her come get you."

Mom stopped at the drugstore on our way home. "Here, suck on one of these," she said when she got back in the car.

I pulled the foil cover off the top of the package, unfolded the wrap from a yellow lozenge, and put it in my mouth. By the time we got home, my throat didn't hurt so much.

"Do you want me to stay with you this afternoon?" Mom asked when she'd parked in front of our house.

"No, I'll be okay. I think I'll go to bed."

"That's a good idea. You ask Mrs. Borg if you want anything. And if you get worse, have her call me at the office. I'll be there until four." Mom gave me a hug before I got out of the car.

I slept all afternoon. Mrs. Borg came in my room just as I opened my eyes. "There's a girl at the door named Missy. She wants to know how you are."

"Tell her I've got a cold."

Mrs. Borg nodded and waddled toward the hall.

"Wait a minute," I said. "Tell her to bring me my health book after school tomorrow. I missed a test."

———

THAT night, for the first time, Jimmy didn't wake up. I slept straight through and slept most of the

55

next day, too. I was up by the time Missy came at three-thirty. "If you don't get close to me, you can come in," I told her.

"No, I just brought your book."

I took the book, wondering why her lips were pursed together and her eyes were scrinched half-shut. I didn't think my cold was that dangerous. "Well, um, thanks," I said.

She started for the stairs and then turned back around to face me. "Why didn't you tell me your teacher's name was Mrs. Shivelly?"

"I thought everybody knew."

"Everybody but me. All I ever heard you and Robert say was Snivelly."

"That's what he nicknamed her. You didn't know that?"

"No, I didn't and it was really embarrassing."

"What was embarrassing?" I asked.

"I went in her room and asked, 'Mrs. Snivelly, could I please have Caitlin's health book?' And she stared at me and said, 'What?' and I said, 'Caitlin's sick, Mrs. Snivelly, and could I please bring—' and she said, 'My name is Mrs. *Shiv*elly.' "

"You didn't! You didn't call her Snivelly." I bent over laughing. It made my throat hurt, but I couldn't stop laughing.

"It wasn't funny, Caitlin."

"I know. I know, but—" And I cracked up again.

"Listen, Caitlin, that was humiliating."

"I know. I know." I tried to straighten myself up, but there was no way.

"I hope you get better soon," Missy snapped and stamped down the steps.

7

BY Monday I felt well enough to go back to school. I met Bones on the sidewalk. He was carrying a large paper sack along with his small lunch bag. "Do you want some raisins?" I asked him. That was the only good thing I'd found in our cupboard.

"Naw, I've got candy." He pulled a Mounds bar out of the sack. Since these bars come in two pieces, I thought he'd give me one. He didn't.

He gobbled up both halves while I popped raisins in my mouth. "What else is in the sack?"

"Clothes," he said.

"Oh, your mom washed your gym shorts?"

He didn't answer that. I didn't think much about it, because lots of times he doesn't answer. Especially if he thinks my question is stupid.

After we got to the end of the block, he jerked his head to the side. "I'm going down this street."

What? I watched him walk toward the gas station on the corner. Why would he want to go down there before school?

I was still wondering that when I crossed over to Missy's house. She wasn't in front, so I went up her steps and knocked on her door. She opened it. "Oh, hi! I was hoping you'd get well before my party. Just a minute. I'll get my books."

I was relieved that she wasn't still mad at me, but she stayed inside more than a minute. I kept checking my watch until she came out. We made it to school in time, though.

Jill and Lindsi rushed up to me when they saw us coming. "Caitlin! You're back," Jill said.

"You look skinnier," Lindsi said.

"I should be," I told her. "It hurt my throat to eat."

They put their arms around me as we walked along the sidewalk to where Robert and Arthur were standing. "Got tired of skipping school, huh?" Robert said.

"No, I got sick of staying home with our babysitter

and her stupid soaps. She can't unglue herself from the TV long enough to change my baby brother's diapers."

"You two should have a lot in common," Arthur said.

I turned on him. "What are you talking about?"

Arthur shrugged. "You said the babysitter's too lazy to work, but I bet she takes the pay."

"Hey, check out Paul Redding over there." Lindsi pointed across the street to the junior high.

Bones was crossing the grass to meet some of his friends.

"Isn't he cute in that denim shirt?" Lindsi asked.

"And jeans that fit, for a change." Jill gave me a smirk. "Now you can walk to school with a dude."

"Ye-es," I said slowly. A strange dude. Fifteen minutes ago, he'd been wearing an old white T-shirt that had been washed about a million times.

The junior high bell must have rung, because Bones, his friends, and the rest of the kids on the lawn moved toward the entrance. I watched until Bones disappeared through the school doors. He was still carrying his large paper sack, but his lunch bag was nowhere in sight.

I BOUGHT a stuffed bear for Missy's birthday. Mom thought that was a ridiculous present for a twelve-year-old girl. She wanted me to get Missy a diary. But the bear had long, silky, golden fur and I thought Missy would love it. And she did.

"Oh, Caitlin," she squealed. "I just love him, love him." She hugged him to her chest. "His name is Beary-Bear."

"He's darling," Jill said.

"Open my present next." Arthur took a small, square package from the pile in the middle of the floor and shoved it at Missy. She was sitting cross-legged in front of her presents. She shifted Beary-Bear to the crook of her elbow and tore the wrappings off Arthur's package.

"A puzzle," she said. "Thanks."

"Here. I'll show you how it works." Arthur grabbed the plastic box out of her hands. "See, you roll these little balls around until they're all in the holes at the same time. It's pretty hard to do. There. Three are in. Now all I have to do is get the fourth one in. See, you roll . . . Darn. Well, you have to keep working on them. There. There. I got it. I got it! See?"

"Good for you," Lindsi said. "Now give Missy back her present."

"I was just showing her." Arthur handed over the puzzle.

Missy put it on the floor and picked up the next package, all the while holding Beary-Bear in her arm. For the first time, I was beginning to really like Missy.

The next present had curly purple ribbons hanging from the pink tissue-paper wrapping. It was from Jill. A diary with a lock.

"That's neat," I said, glad I hadn't gotten her one.

After all the presents were opened, we had the pizza. Mrs. Mitchell served it on paper plates in the dining room. I was wondering where Mr. Mitchell was. Arthur was, too. "When's your dad showing up?"

"In a little while," Missy said. "One of his patients broke her arm and she's allergic to pain pills, so Dad's taking the pain away for her."

"He can do that?" Robert asked.

"Of course," Missy said.

Mr. Mitchell did show up just as we were finishing off the cake. "Didn't you save me a piece?" he asked Missy's mom, as Robert helped himself to the last wedge.

Robert turned red and dropped the cake back on the serving plate.

"No, no. Take it, Robert," Mrs. Mitchell said and then turned to her husband. "Of course I saved a piece for you, dear. It's on the counter in the kitchen."

While her dad ate, Missy took all of us into the living room. She perched on the davenport and had us face her in a half circle on the floor. That was so we all could see her being hypnotized, she said.

When Mr. Mitchell came in, he sat next to Missy. He's a tall, thin man with glasses and hardly any hair.

I was thinking that neither of her parents had wiry, bushy, curly hair like Missy and then I remembered she was adopted.

"Let's see now." Mr. Mitchell rubbed his hands back and forth on his trouser legs. "I guess you all need to be quiet until I'm finished and then I'll try to answer your questions. Missy, are you comfortable? Maybe we'd better put a pillow behind you."

She settled back against the pillow, and Mr. Mitchell said in an ordinary voice, "Now, I want you to take a deep breath and close your eyes."

Missy took a deep breath and closed her eyes.

"Open your eyes. Now this time when you close them, you will feel twice as relaxed as you were before."

Missy opened and closed her eyes.

"Now, take another deep breath. Breathe slowly while you feel the muscles around your eyes relax. Relax them until they won't work. When you are certain they won't work, try them to be sure they won't work."

I could see Missy wiggle the skin around her eyes, but they didn't open.

"Let that feeling of relaxation go down through your body until it reaches your toes. Feel yourself covered with a warm blanket of relaxation."

I was imagining a warm blanket over me and was beginning to feel pretty loose myself. Mr. Mitchell told Missy he was going to lift her hand and it would be as droopy as a noodle. He lifted her hand and her arm waggled back and forth like a dead man's.

Arthur was sitting on one side of me stroking his chin with his fingers. I could see by the way his lower lip pouched out that he didn't believe in hypnotism yet.

Mr. Mitchell told Missy that her body was relaxed and now he wanted her mind relaxed. He had her pretend that she was going down a long flight of stairs. As she went down each step, he made her more and more drowsy, sleepier and sleepier. By the time she reached the bottom, she was so out of it that drool was leaking from the side of her mouth.

"I'm going to put a needle in your hand, Missy. You will feel a very slight prick when I do. And you will remain relaxed and comfortable."

This sat me up straight. And all the other kids, too. Missy just lolled back on her pillow while her dad took a vial and an envelope of pads out of his jacket pocket. He wiped a pad across the skin between Missy's thumb and index finger. I guessed that was to sterilize it.

He slipped the needle out of the vial. Jill was sitting on the other side of me and I heard her suck in a breath. I was holding mine.

"I'm going to prick your skin with a needle now,

Missy." He was holding her thumb with his left hand. With his other hand, he threaded the needle right through the webbed piece of skin at the base of her thumb.

"Jeez," Robert said.

Arthur's head was jutted forward and his mouth was hanging open as he stared at the needle that was sticking out both sides of Missy's hand. I gave him a poke, "Believe it now?"

He scowled at me. "Shh!"

"Missy, I'm going to remove the needle," Mr. Mitchell said. "Your skin will heal itself instantly."

I watched to see if there was any blood when he pulled the needle out. There wasn't. He said that when she woke up she would be happy, healthy, and full of energy. He said if anyone else tried to hypnotize her, she would remain awake and alert.

Mr. Mitchell had Missy count from one to five, telling her that her eyes would open at the count of five. They did. She smiled at all of us. I thought she looked happy and healthy, all right.

"Does your hand hurt?" Jill asked.

Missy looked at her thumb. "No."

"Didn't you feel anything at all when your dad stuck the needle in you?" Robert wanted to know.

"I felt a prick," Missy said. "I knew he was sticking it in, but I didn't feel any pain."

"What I don't understand," Robert said to Mr. Mitchell, "is why you didn't just come out and tell Missy she wouldn't feel any pain."

Mr. Mitchell nodded. "That's a good question. The reason I didn't is because negatives don't register on the subconscious mind. If I said she would *not* feel pain, the suggestion she'd receive is that she would feel pain."

"Hmm, tricky," Robert said.

Arthur got to his feet and went over to stand by Mr. Mitchell. "Can I give it a try on Missy?"

Mr. Mitchell laughed. "No. When Missy was in her trance, I gave her the suggestion that no one else could hypnotize her. That protects her from being hypnotized by anyone who doesn't know what he's doing."

"But you could teach me," Arthur said, "so I'd know what I was doing."

"I'm afraid that would take a long time and you would have to be licensed."

"Rats, there's always a catch," Arthur said and sat down.

"I will show you all one thing." Mr. Mitchell folded his hands between his long legs and leaned toward us. "I'll show you how a stage hypnotist chooses the people he wants to come on stage and work with him. Okay?"

"Sure," Robert said.

"All of you put your finger on your forehead and

close your eyes. Make an imaginary imprint by pressing your finger into your forehead."

I did. I pressed my finger into the middle of my forehead.

"Keeping your eyes closed, look up at the imprint. Look up. Look up."

I was looking up as hard as I could.

"Now, keep looking up," Mr. Mitchell instructed, "and try to open your eyes."

I tried. And tried. And tried. They didn't open.

"What's the catch?" I heard Arthur say beside me.

Mr. Mitchell must have ignored him. "Take your fingers down and open your eyes."

I took my finger down and my eyes popped open.

"Did you hypnotize us?" Arthur asked in an accusing voice.

"No, I didn't," Mr. Mitchell said calmly. "Now all of you squeeze your eyes closed."

I squeezed mine closed.

"Squeeze harder and harder. Squeeze as hard as you can. While you are squeezing, try opening your eyes."

I tried. They didn't open.

"Okay," he said. "You can stop squeezing and open your eyes."

We did.

"Put your hands out like this and lock your fingers." Mr. Mitchell extended his arms in front of him and laced his fingers together. We all imitated him.

"Lock your fingers together as tightly as you can. Squeeze. Squeeze harder. Harder. Squeeze until your knuckles are white. You won't be able to take your hands apart now. Try it and see."

I tried, but my hands didn't come loose. I looked over at Arthur. His split apart. So did Lindsi's. Then Robert's. I pulled harder and finally Jill's and my hands fell open at the same time.

"What's going on?" Arthur asked.

Mr. Mitchell smiled. "What's going on is suggestion. When I told you to look up and open your eyes, you couldn't. That's because the muscles for looking up are the same ones you use for opening your eyes. And you use the same muscles for squeezing your eyes shut as you do for opening them. Of course you couldn't do both at the same time.

"When I told you you couldn't unlock your hands, some of you believed you couldn't do that either. You were responding to suggestion. A stage hypnotist would choose the ones who had the hardest time pulling their hands apart. He'd ask them to come on stage, because he'd know he could hypnotize them quickly."

"Those are the dumb ones," Arthur said smugly.

"Oh, no. On the contrary. People who can be hypnotized easily are generally more intelligent than the average population."

"Wha-at?" Arthur said.

I gave him a hard jab this time. "Ye-es, Arthur."

68

8

WHEN I got home, I was so excited about the party that I babbled away to Mom about it. She was sitting at the kitchen table filling out insurance forms. She barely paid attention until I got to the needle part.

Then she put down her pen and looked up at me with a horrified expression on her face. "Do you mean he stuck a needle in his own daughter?"

"Yes, but it didn't hurt her or anything."

"You just told me you saw the needle threaded through her thumb."

Ohh, this was not good. "Not her thumb, Mom. It

was the skin between her thumb and index finger."

"Either way, you can't make me believe that wouldn't hurt her. And she could get infected."

"No, no. He wiped her off with an antiseptic pad and it was a new needle in a glass tube. It wasn't dangerous at all."

"Did he hypnotize you or any of the other kids?" Mom's tone gave me visions of Mr. Mitchell being dragged away by the cops.

"Of course not. And he wouldn't even tell us how to do it."

"What difference would it make if he told you? He showed all of you, didn't he?"

"Mom, calm down. You're just getting excited for nothing. It was a party and he was trying to entertain us."

"Well, I don't like you seeing that kind of entertainment. I don't know if you should be going over there any—"

Jimmy's howls filled the house. "I'll get him," I said quickly.

Mom got up from the table. "No, stay here. *I'll* get him."

She marched out of the kitchen as if she had to protect Jimmy from being contaminated by me. I should never have mentioned hypnosis.

My sister Susan came for dinner the next night. She thinks Mom gets lonesome when Dad's on the road. I think it's my sister who gets lonesome. Mom has me and Jimmy, but my sister lives in an apartment all by herself.

Susan played with Jimmy until dinner was ready. During dinner, Mom brought up the levy the school district was proposing. "I realize new people are moving in and teachers shouldn't have forty kids in a classroom, but . . ." Mom paused to shake her head. "It means more taxes."

"Is the levy going to be on the ballot?" Susan asked.

"I don't know. There's going to be a board meeting at the junior high at noon tomorrow. I'm trying to arrange my schedule so I can go."

"I bet Mrs. Redding will be there," I put in.

Mom laughed. "I bet you're right."

After dinner, Mom made some calls and Susan came upstairs with me. While we put Jimmy to bed, I told her about Mr. Mitchell hypnotizing Missy.

"That must have been fascinating to watch," Susan said. "I have a friend who weighed two hundred pounds. She went to a hypnotist and he found out why she ate and helped her lose sixty-five pounds."

"Your friend weighed two hundred pounds?!" I said. "She must have been a monster."

"Well, she didn't look too hot in a bathing suit. But listen, Caitlin, I wouldn't talk about hypnosis around Mom. That kind of thing scares her."

"I already told her and she freaked out good. She almost said I couldn't go over to Missy's house anymore."

My sister raised her eyebrows. "Big mistake, honey. Don't bring up the subject again. She's got so much on her mind, she'll probably forget about it."

"I hope," I said.

BONES carried his big sack and small lunch bag to school in the morning. I didn't say anything about his changing clothes every day. I did say something about his lunch disappearing.

We were about half a block from our houses and a little spotted dog was following us. Bones took out one of his sandwiches and tossed it to the dog. "Here, pooch, have some chow."

This dog was no Wigger. It stopped long enough to gulp down the sandwich and then was on Bones's heels again. "Still hungry, huh? Here, have some more." Bones gave his second sandwich to the dog and then wadded up the empty bag and put it in his big sack.

"What are you going to eat for lunch?" I asked him.

"I buy my lunch now. Supers." The way he said it was almost bragging. He was obviously proud of having money to buy big lunches. But where was he getting the money? Not from his mother, that was for sure.

He left me at the corner to go down to the gas station. I worried about him all the way to school.

Even when Missy was showing off her birthday earrings, I was still worrying.

By the morning recess, though, Bones got shoved into the back of my mind. Arthur was running around trying to talk somebody into letting him hypnotize them. I told him, "No way."

So did Lindsi. He finally got Jill to do it. Jill's so easygoing, she'll do about anything you ask her.

Arthur took her to the edge of the playfield and smashed down the grass. "Sit here," he said. "You can lean against the bank."

Jill tried to settle back, but there was a rock behind her. Arthur bustled over and pulled it out of the ground. He patted more grass into the hole it left. "There. Now, are you comfortable?"

Jill squirmed around until she was.

"Lean your head back and close your eyes. Open your eyes. Now, when you close them again, you will be twice as relaxed. Relax all your muscles. Relax the muscles around your eyes. They are not going to work. Try them so you know they won't work."

Jill must have tried because her eyes snapped open behind her thick glasses. Lindsi and I were standing behind Arthur. We both clapped our hands over our mouths at the same time.

"Come on, Jill," Arthur said. "It isn't fair unless you really try."

"I'm trying," Jill said.

"Take a deep breath and close your eyes. Feel yourself all relaxed. Let that feeling go down you, until it touches your toes. Feel a blanket of relaxation go all over your body." Arthur was talking in this slow, deep voice. I looked at Lindsi and bursts of giggles split through our fingers. Arthur turned to glare at us before he droned on.

"Now, I'm going to lift your hand and it will be droopy as a noodle." Arthur lifted Jill's hand. He wagged it back and forth. It was easy to see Jill was wagging it along with him.

"Let your muscles go limp. Limp. Very limp. Your muscles will be limp."

Jill took her hand away from Arthur and scratched her back. "This grass itches."

That was when the bell rang. We three girls followed Arthur as he stamped back into the building.

Mrs. Shivelly announced our spelling test. I'd forgotten all about it. While I was getting my pen and paper out of my desk, I frantically tried to remember how to spell *kneel*, *knead*, and *gnaw*. I thought all of them started with a *k*, but I wasn't sure.

"This is a test on silent letters." Mrs. Shivelly stood in front of the room with her teacher's spelling book in her hand. "The first word is *kiln*. I put the clay pot into the kiln. *Kiln*."

That had a silent *n* on the end of it. I remembered that.

"*Knead.* Mother will knead the dough. *Knead. Knowledge.* He has a great deal of knowledge. *Knowledge. Psychology.* He studied psychology in college. *Psychology.*"

I was doing great. Silent *k's* and silent *p's.* Then came *gnaw* and *gnarl.* I spelled them with a *k.* That didn't look right. I erased the *k,* but that left the words without a silent letter. How do you spell *gnaw?*

I sneaked a look at Arthur's side of the desk. He had his back turned to me and his arm curled around his paper, of course. Mrs. Shivelly was on *scent* and *scissors.* Silent *c.* I wrote those words down in a hurry.

Arthur sneezed, yanked a tissue out of his pants pocket, and blew his nose. I got in a quick glance at his paper. *G!* That was it. I ignored Arthur's dirty look and put a *g* before my *naw* and *narl.* Now I'd get an A for sure.

After we passed in our papers, Mrs. Shivelly gave us time for free reading. The one good part of school. I was almost at the end of *The Red Pony,* which I love.

I finished my book before the period was over and sat looking out the window. A gray car went up the street and then came back down. The driver was probably searching for a parking place. That board meeting Mom talked about must be going on at the junior high.

The gray car pulled into our parking lot. A lady got out. Oh, it was Mrs. Redding in her old gray Rabbit. Mrs. Redding! I sat up straight. Mrs. Redding might pass Bones in the junior high hallway. And Bones would be wearing his new clothes, which Mrs. Redding had no doubt never seen.

I slipped my thumbnail back and forth between my teeth. How was I going to warn Bones? How was I ever going to do it?

What time did Bones have lunch? What time? I knew the junior high had two lunches. I seemed to remember that Bones had the second one. That would mean he'd be finished eating and be walking around the halls about a quarter to one or one. If the board had a noon meeting, did that mean they'd be through at one o'clock?

I checked my watch. It was three minutes to twelve. If I was right, Bones should be in the junior high cafetorium at twelve-thirty. I could ask Jill to cover for me during our noon recess. She'd do it, but she'd also tell Lindsi. And they'd want to know all about Bones and his sack and his new clothes and his old clothes.

It would be better if I could sneak over to the junior high by myself. Maybe I could say I was going to the library and then zip out the front doors. Maybe—

"Put your books away, clear off your desks, and fold your hands so I know you are ready for lunch," Mrs. Shively said.

9

MY heart was beating fast as we lined up to go out for lunch recess. It beat even faster when I said to Jill, "I just remembered. I have to get a book in the library. I'll meet you guys outside in a few minutes."

Before Jill or Lindsi could say anything, I dashed down the hall and around the corner to wait until my class was on the playground. Then I scuttled back along the wall like a crab. I crept past the office, checked around quickly, and dived out the front doors.

I ran across the street so fast I didn't even see the

car. I just yelled, "Shut up," at the blasting horn. I was breathless by the time I reached the junior high. After yanking those doors open, I started down the main hall. There were kids everywhere, most of them bigger than I was.

A sign by the office window announced: BOARD MEETING—BAND ROOM—112. I didn't know where that was. I didn't know exactly where the cafetorium was either. It'd been two years since my fourth grade teacher had taken us to see a play in there.

I went up to three girls who were standing by a dance poster. "Where's the cafetorium?"

"That way." The girl with red heart earrings pointed toward the back of the building.

I saw the double doors leading to the cafetorium as soon as I got to the end of the hall. The place was packed inside. There were lines for hamburgers, lines for milkshakes, lines for salad. Bones wasn't in any of them.

I walked through the middle of the room, looking at each table. The place smelled of old bananas and orange peels. There were so many tables and so many kids, I almost gave up hope.

Someone yelled, "Heads up!" and a blob of jello flew from one table to another. An apple zipped back. A man with a crew cut marched toward the action and I faded to the back wall.

I must have stood there five minutes, turning my

head this way and that, watching every boy who came in and left. Suddenly I spotted his black hair. He was leaving with two of his friends.

"Bones!" I hollered, before I thought.

Two kids turned around on their bench to stare at me. I hurried across the room and grabbed Bones's shirt just before he went out the doors. He did a double take. "What are you doing here?"

"I have to talk to you." Luckily, you don't have to explain much to Bones, because I was running out of recess time.

He told his friends he'd catch them later, pulled me over to a window, and asked, "Okay, what's up?"

"Your mom's at the board meeting and it will get out pretty soon."

"Here?"

"Yes, in the band room."

Bones's eyes shifted to the window for a second, then he said, "Thanks," and was gone.

I weaved in and out of the crowds in the hall, making my way back to the front entrance. I zipped across the street and into the elementary school just as the bell rang, ending recess. Pretending that I'd been in the library the whole time, I strolled casually into my classroom. Mrs. Shively looked up from her desk, but didn't say anything.

When the kids straggled in from the playground, Jill stopped by my desk. "You didn't come out."

79

"No," I said. "I got stuck shelving books for Mr. Lewis."

———

AFTER school, I hurried Missy out of the building and down the street. "What's up?" she asked.

"I wanna see Bones," I said. "And he'll be somewhere ahead of us."

I don't think Missy's as athletic as I am. She was puffing by the time I caught sight of Bones across the street and down the block. He was wearing his old clothes and carrying his paper sack. He must have kept them in his locker and changed in the boys' bathroom after I warned him.

When I slowed down, Missy gave me a funny look. "I thought you wanted to talk to him."

"No," I said. "I only wanted to see him."

"You're weird, you know. Listen, can you have dinner with me and stay over Friday night? My dad keeps his office open until nine on Fridays. Mom will let us order pizza or fried chicken and she'll rent a movie for us to watch until they get home."

"Sounds good, but I'll have to ask first." I wasn't too sure of what Mom'd say. She hadn't had much time to forget about the hypnosis.

I waited until she'd eaten dinner and was relaxing in the living room with her coffee before I brought it up. She frowned anyway. "I don't know if I want you spending a whole lot of time over there."

"Mom, Missy's dad has a clinic and her mother is the secretary. They do weight loss and stuff. It's just like any other office."

"Well, all right. Only the next time you two plan an overnight, you have Missy stay here."

"She'll be glad to," I agreed.

On Friday night, Missy and I ordered fried chicken. By the time they delivered it, the mashed potatoes were cold but the rest of the dinner was good. "What's the name of the movie?" I wanted to know.

"*Bull Durham*. Mom said it's a comedy about baseball."

The movie was funny, all right, but I don't think Mrs. Mitchell had ever seen it. She must have chosen it by the picture on the front of the cassette.

When one actress asked the other what the baseball player had said to the umpire, I asked Missy the same thing. "Just a minute," she said. "We'll roll the tape back."

We played it twice before we got it. We played the bedroom scenes twice, too. We were sitting on the flowered couch. The girl in the movie tied the pitcher's hands to the bedpost, and Missy and I flopped onto the floor giggling.

"That was the best show," I said, while Missy rewound the film.

"Ya, it was good." She put the cassette on top of the TV. "Let's feed Wigger the chicken bones."

"I don't think you're supposed to give a dog chicken bones. The splinters might pierce his stomach."

"No they won't," Missy said. "His big jaws will mash the bones to a pulp."

"Only maybe. And how come I keep smelling roses? Is that you?"

"Yes." She smiled, pleased with herself. "It's my mom's new perfume. You want to try it? Come on in her bedroom."

The bedroom was about what I expected. Matching shiny gold curtains and bedspread. The only messy thing in the room was a black phone, its attachments, and a tangle of wires piled on a chair.

Missy sprayed my neck with the perfume from her mom's dresser. "You want some on your wrists too?" she asked.

"No, that's enough." I pointed to the chair. "Is that a cellular phone?"

"It's a car phone my dad got. He's having it installed in his car."

"How come he didn't keep it in a box?"

"I don't know." She put the perfume back on the dresser. "Let's go feed Wigger."

I shook my head. "I still don't think it's a good idea."

But my objections never stop Missy. Once she gets started on a plan, she just keeps going. She marched out of the bedroom, grabbed a handful of bones off her plate on the bar, and went for the back door.

I sighed and tagged after her.

She barely had the door open, when we heard the yelling. "You're a moron! You're a moron! You're a complete moron!" It was Bob Dorman yelling at his brother Derek. They were standing near the end of their shed. We could just make them out through the dusk.

Missy quietly sat down on her porch step and yanked on my jeans so I'd sit down beside her.

"How'd I know the horn was going to start honking?" Derek's voice was whiny.

"Because, stupid, every Mercedes comes with a car alarm."

"Well, I would have gotten that deck out fast."

A sharp *thump* clapped through the night. I jumped. "Did Bob hit him?" I whispered to Missy.

"I think he hit the shed with his fist. Shh," she warned.

"You are so stupid!" Bob Dorman sounded as if he were going crazy. "Stupid! If you try to rip out a radio and deck in a Mercedes they self-destruct. You almost got us busted for nothing."

"How was I supposed to know? Nobody told me."

Derek must be dumb, I decided, because he acted about four years old.

"Well, from now on, all you're going to be is a look-out," Bob said. "That just takes a pair of eyes. It doesn't take brains. And you better not screw that up. If you do, you're on your own."

"I won't screw it up, Bob."

Bob disappeared around the end of the shed with Derek after him. There was the bang of the shed door closing. A pause. Then car doors slammed twice, a motor roared, and the sound of a car leaving the alley faded away.

"They're rip offs," I told Missy.

"Right," Missy said. "That's what I thought they were. I can hardly wait to see what they've got in their shed."

"They've obviously got hot car decks and radios. Why do you need to see them? You probably should tell your dad."

"No, he always accuses me of imagining things. I'm going to have proof before I say anything to him." She jumped down the rest of the steps and went over to the fence. "Here, boy. Here, Wigger. Chicken. Smell?"

I could tell Wigger wasn't smelling because the fat white blur ten feet inside the fence didn't move. "You're not going to get him to come," I said.

"I will when he gets used to me." She threw the bones at Wigger.

The blur moved, there were two crunches, and silence. "He swallowed them whole," I said.

She walked back up to the porch. "No, he didn't. He chewed them."

I followed Missy into her house, hoping Wigger wouldn't be dead in the morning.

10

WHEN I got home from Missy's on Saturday afternoon, Dad was home. He wanted me to change my clothes because we were going out to dinner with his boss. "Wear that dark blue blouse of yours," he said. "It makes your eyes look purple."

"Purple! I don't want purple eyes."

"Violet eyes then." He put his arm around me and walked me to the stairs. "And don't wear those dirty Keds."

I looked down at my feet. "These aren't Keds and

they're not dirty. They just have grass stains on them."

He ruffled my hair. "Look pretty."

I went up to my room, took a shower, and put on the blue blouse, white jeans, and sandals. "That's my girl," Dad said when I came downstairs.

"I thought I was your girl," Mom said. She was sitting on the couch across from Dad. Jimmy was on the floor by her feet practicing his rollovers.

I dropped down beside him. "I hope Mrs. Borg changes his pants while we're gone."

Dad frowned at Mom. "Doesn't she change his diapers?"

"Of course she does," Mom said.

"Sure. Every day. About five minutes before you come home." I didn't look at her. I kept looking at Jimmy. I knew this was going to make her mad.

It did.

"You're exaggerating, Caitlin," she snapped.

"No, I'm not. And I'm not exaggerating the rash all over his bottom, either."

"There are lots of reasons for a baby's rash." Mom's voice was even sharper. "It can be caused by something innocent like carrots."

Or Mrs. Borg, I was about to say. But just then she knocked on our door. Dad let her in. She took off her sweater and bustled over to Jimmy as if he were her one great love.

She held Jimmy while Mom told her we'd be at Rover's restaurant in Seattle and she was to call if anything went wrong.

"Oh, I'm sure it won't," Mrs. Borg said.

Dad and I were standing by the front door next to Mom. He waited until Mom was finished before he told Mrs. Borg, "Be sure Jimmy always has dry pants."

"Oh, yes," Mom added, "and use the Baby Wipes each time you change him."

Mrs. Borg gave my parents a superior little smile. "Well, it isn't like the old days. The new plastic diapers keep urine away from the baby's sensitive skin."

"Not if there's a puddle in the bottom of the diaper," I said.

Mrs. Borg's smile faded. I was no favorite of hers.

"We'd better be going." Mom opened the door. "Call us if you need us."

"And be careful about leaving wet diapers on Jimmy," Dad added.

"Oh, no," Mrs. Borg said hurriedly. "I never do."

Liar, I thought to myself.

On the trip to Seattle, I sat in the backseat of our car. Mom ignored me by talking insurance with Dad until she gradually got their twosome tight again. I kept my mouth shut while she did it. It's in my best interest to have her in a good mood. Especially since I'd taken care of Mrs. Borg.

You have to drive through the Seattle arboretum

and by Washington Park on the way to Rover's. I was staring out the window at the banks of rhododendrons when Dad turned his head toward me. "After you take a roll, break off one piece and butter it. After you finish that, you can break off another piece and butter it. I've seen you butter your whole roll."

I didn't say anything. It makes more sense to butter the whole roll, but whatever.

"And," he said, "you scoop your spoon away from you when you eat soup."

"I'm going to have salad."

"That's fine. I just thought I'd tell you." He went back to his driving and didn't pay any more attention to me until he'd parked in front of Rover's. Then he gave me a quick appraisal as we got out of the car.

"Are my teeth on straight?" I asked him.

"You're perfect," he said.

Rover's is in a house on a side road off Madison. Mom brushed the wrinkles out of her skirt as we went through the garden gate and up the steps. Dad held the door open to the reception room. On the other side of that, I could see Dad's boss, Jason, and his wife, Johanna, at a table.

Jason jumped up to greet us. He's handsome and bigger than my dad. Johanna's tiny with long black hair and huge brown eyes. There was a wine bottle on the table. Jason filled glasses for Mom and Dad. His glass was already full.

"You aren't having any?" Mom asked Johanna.

Johanna patted her stomach.

"When?" Mom said.

"December."

"You're going to have a baby?" I asked.

Johanna smiled and nodded to me. The waiter gave us menus and she ordered a house salad to start her dinner and so did I. Everyone else had a spinach salad.

When the waiter put the plate of curly greens and flower petals in front of Johanna, her eyes grew round. "What's the matter?" Jason asked.

As soon as the waiter left, Johanna whispered, "I can't eat the pansy."

"Here." Jason picked the pansy off the top of her salad and tucked it in her hair.

I didn't have the nerve to put my nasturtium behind my ear, but I wanted to. I pushed it to the side of my dish. While we were eating, the pony-tailed chef came through the rooms, greeting people.

He stopped at a table next to ours. "Are you the chef?" a gray-haired lady asked him.

"It depends on whether or not you liked your dinner," he said.

I thought he was funny. He and Dad rattled off French together. The only thing I could understand of that was *Bon! Bon!* Good! Good! Especially the dessert. A creamy custard with raspberry sauce in red scallops around the plate.

90

I described it all to Missy when she came over the next morning. "But why," Missy asked, "wouldn't the boss's wife eat the pansy?"

"Because she loves flowers and wouldn't want to hurt one."

"Weird," Missy said. "The flower was going to die anyway."

There are some things that Missy just doesn't get. She wanted to talk about Wigger anyway.

"Listen, he comes up to the fence now. If we work on him today, we should be able to pet him."

"I don't know," I said. "Mom would like you to visit here as much as I visit your house."

Missy shook her kinky hair impatiently. "Your folks are downstairs glued to the TV. They aren't even going to look up until the Mariners game is over. All you have to do is walk right by them saying you're going over to my house to play and you'll be home for dinner. They always like that 'home for dinner' part. I use it all the time."

"We-ell, okay. I'll try it."

We went downstairs and as I passed Mom, I said, "I'm going over to Missy's to play. I'll be home for dinner."

She nodded and Missy and I sailed out the door.

"See, it works," Missy said. "Never ask them. Tell them where you're going and when you'll be home. That keeps them from being nervous."

We crossed the street at the corner and saw Mr. Kager strolling down the sidewalk toward us. He was whistling happily and swinging a cane. As we passed him, he tipped his hat and said, "Good afternoon, girls."

Mrs. Kager came dashing down the block after him. She tore by us and grabbed his arm. "What are you doing? I've been looking all over for you!"

He backed up a bit. "Calm down, woman. I'm just out for a walk."

She stared at us for a second and then whirled frantically back to him. "You must never forget to take me with you."

Missy and I moved on to her house. We could hear Mrs. Kager behind us, repeating and repeating, "Don't ever forget to take me with you again."

"Do you know those people?" Missy asked, climbing up her steps ahead of me.

"That's Mr. and Mrs. Kager. He's crazy."

"He looks okay to me. She's the one who sounds crazy."

"Ya, well he told me he flies over houses."

Missy's parents were in the living room making up a flyer advertising their clinic. Mrs. Mitchell said hello, but Mr. Mitchell frowned at Missy. "Is your room cleaned up?"

"Almost," Missy said. "Caitlin can only stay a little while so I'll finish cleaning it after she leaves."

"I thought we agreed that you wouldn't do anything or go anywhere until your room was in order." Mr. Mitchell's voice was firm.

Mrs. Mitchell put her hand on his arm. "Oh, honey, let her entertain her guest now that she's here. Missy can get her room cleaned before dinner."

Mr. Mitchell's frown deepened, but he didn't say any more. We scurried into the kitchen where Missy lifted a hunk of cheese out of the refrigerator.

"Doesn't your mom miss all the stuff you swipe?" I asked her.

"No," Missy said. "She shops on the way home from work and forgets what she has. I usually empty the grocery bags."

Str-range family!

We went out in the backyard to call Wigger. Just like Missy said, he came right to the fence. He liked cheese, too. Long ropes of slobber hung from his flabby jowls while he waited for Missy to break off a piece.

"Good, good, isn't it, Wigger?" Missy crooned.

More drool dripped off Wigger while his little round eyes fastened on the hunk of cheese in Missy's hand.

Each time she poked a piece through the wire, he came closer until she had him licking it right off her fingers. "Here," she said, handing me what was left of the chunk. "You feed him now."

I cautiously held a bit of cheese close to the fence.

Wigger slipped his pink tongue through an opening and licked it up.

"See," Missy said. "He isn't scary. Now do it slowly this time so I can pet him."

I fed him slowly and Missy petted his head. Wigger seemed to like the petting almost as much as the cheese. He moved his head around so Missy could scratch his ears. "You're a sweetie pie," Missy told him.

Wigger stood still for more scratches even after the cheese was gone. "Pet him," Missy said to me.

I petted him.

"We could get into the shed Friday night if you can stay over," Missy suggested.

"I don't know. How can we be sure the Dormans won't be home?"

"Simple. Mrs. Dorman reads in the evening. We can see her lamp through the windows. She can't hear anything, remember. And if the car isn't here, the guys aren't here."

"I don't know. I don't know if my mom will go for it." I wasn't sure I did either.

"I'll tell you what." Missy's hair bounced up and down with each nod. "I'll come over to your house every day after school until your mom's sick of seeing me. Then, when you tell her you're spending Friday night with me, she'll be glad. And we'll order pizza this time."

The pizza did it. I agreed to her crazy plan. She hunched her shoulders together and flattened her lips, giggling in anticipation. "It's such a good joke on the Dormans. Thinking they've got their shed guarded by that pussycat dog."

ON the way to school Monday morning, I couldn't resist. I told Bones about Missy making friends with Wigger. Bones's jaw hardened, so I knew he wasn't pleased.

"Missy thinks Wigger's a pussycat," I added.

"Missy's dingy," he said.

That's what I thought, too, but I didn't tell Bones. I didn't tell him about her plan to go over the fence and investigate the shed, either. Instead, I asked him about the wooden thing he was carrying with his clothes sack.

He shook it and it clacked.

"But what is it?"

"It's a primitive musical instrument." Bones held it up for me to see. The instrument was carved out of dark wood. It had a narrow handle with four oblong pieces loosely screwed to the top.

"It looks like a rattle," I said. "Jimmy'd like that."

"No, it might poison him if he chewed on it. I had to varnish it for shop."

I hadn't really meant for him to *give* it to Jimmy,

but Bones must have been thinking about that seriously. He said, "After the shop teacher grades it, I'll sand the varnish off. You can come over tomorrow and get it."

I didn't tell him Missy'd be at my house. I was hoping to leave her there while I ran over to Bones's. So Tuesday after school, I suggested that she stay with Mrs. Borg and play with Jimmy while I picked up the rattle. No way. She had to come along.

We found him sitting on a stool in the basement sanding every last smear of varnish off the inside of the clackers. Anything that Bones does has to be perfect.

While I waited for him to finish, Missy wandered around the basement. There were cement washtubs on one wall and on another wall were shelves holding jars of pink-colored rhubarb and cream-colored applesauce. Mrs. Redding must have made the sauce from the apples Bones and I picked for her.

A tall cabinet next to the tubs had no doorknobs. "What's locked up in here?" Missy asked Bones.

"Beats me," he said.

She pried her fingers into the middle crack. The door opened. "Hey, it's not locked."

There was nothing in the cabinet but a gray metal box. Bones stared at it with narrowed eyes.

Missy took down the box from the top shelf. A key was sticking out the front of it. "This is weird," she said. "Why would someone leave a key in a strongbox?"

I waited for Bones to tell her to mind her own business. He didn't. She held the box with one hand, turned the key with the other, then tilted the insides toward us. The box was empty. "What was this used for?" she asked.

"Good question," he said and lowered his head to concentrate on his sanding.

I knew Bones and I knew he knew what had been in that box. "You've looked in there before," I said.

"No," he said slowly, "that cabinet used to be locked."

"Used to be locked?" Missy said. "Why would your mom keep a cabinet locked when you're the only one who lives with her?"

And that was a good question, too, I thought.

"Here." Bones handed me the rattle. "Your brother can chew on this now."

I took the rattle from him and ran my fingers over the handle. "You've made it silky smooth. Don't you want to come see Jimmy play with it?"

"You can do that." Bones slid off his stool and walked across the basement with me.

Missy shoved the box back on the top shelf and caught up with us. As I opened the door, I said to Bones, "Why don't you fix that squeak?"

"I've tried," he said. "We have to get new hinges."

"Your mother will pay for those?"

"Not a chance."

I walked a few steps outside with Missy before I turned back to him. "Thanks for giving Jimmy the rattle. He'll love it."

Jimmy did. He waved it in the air and laughed when it clacked. He dropped it on the floor and cried for me to pick it up. He gummed it until it was soaking wet.

Missy got tired of watching him, so she curled up in a chair and flipped through a magazine. "Did you clean up your room after I left the other night?" I asked her.

"No, I stalled around until it was time for me to go to bed and then Mom helped me. Actually, she did most of it."

"Didn't that make your dad mad?"

"Sure, but he gets over it."

My mom came home about then and smiled when she saw Jimmy on my lap playing with the rattle. "What a pretty toy," she said. "Where did you get it?"

"Bones made it," I said proudly.

11

FRIDAY evening came faster than I wanted. I think I was half hoping I'd never have to investigate the shed. If Missy's mom got sick or the Dorman brothers were home, I'd be saved from chickening out.

Unluckily for me, the Dormans' car was gone when I got to Missy's house about five o'clock. "The coast is clear," she announced as soon as I came in the door.

"But Mrs. Dorman might see us," I said.

"Oh, we'll wait until dark. Dad closes at nine, but it'll take them an hour to shut up the clinic and drive home."

I sat down on Missy's couch and slid my thumbnail back and forth through my front teeth. This annoys my mom and when I noticed what I was doing, I stopped.

Missy had flopped into a chair sideways and was swinging her legs over the arm. "Dad picked up *Little Big Man* for us. Should we watch it before we order the pizza? Or should we order first?"

"Let's order first."

The pizza was prime. Canadian bacon and pineapple. We ate the whole thing. The movie was good, too. But parts of it were sad. I covered my eyes so I couldn't see Little Big Man's pretty Indian wife slaughtered.

Missy didn't seem to mind. She kept her eyes open all the way through. "Well, that's it," she said when it was over. "Now for the big event!"

My stomach sank. "What about Mrs. Dorman?"

Missy peered out her living-room window. "Her lamp's on. She's reading."

"I hope she doesn't get up to go to the bathroom."

"It doesn't matter if she does. She can't hear anything, so she won't look outside." Missy headed for the kitchen. "I'll get my dad's flashlight and some cheese."

I tagged after her. I knew I was doing too much tagging. I knew I should have had the nerve to say I didn't want to get caught snooping in somebody's shed. But part of me didn't want to get left out. And part of me didn't want Missy mad at me for saying no.

So I trailed after her, mumbling that maybe Mrs. Dorman couldn't hear, but she could see. She might see the beam from the flashlight. Missy brushed this off by saying we wouldn't turn the light on until we got to the shed.

Missy climbed the fence first. I watched her go up and ease down to the other side. When Wigger came over to sniff her, she patted his head and gave him the piece of cheese. "Gimme the flashlight," she told me. I poked it through the wires. She hadn't wanted to carry it while she was climbing.

"Well, come on," she said.

I climbed up, teetered at the top, let go, and hit the ground with a jolt that jarred my teeth. Missy didn't wait for me to get my balance. She headed for the shed with Wigger on her heels. It wasn't quite dark. We could still see our way across the yard.

"Rats," she said, rattling the shed door. "It's padlocked."

Good, I thought to myself.

"Hmm, I guess I better get Dad's hammer." She took off to the fence again, hauled herself over the top, and disappeared into the dusk. A few seconds later, she was back at the fence, dropping the hammer through the wires, and climbing over. By this time,

Wigger had figured out that he wasn't going to get any more treats and trotted off to lie down under his tree.

I thought Missy was going to pound on the padlock, but instead she used the claw end of the hammer to wrench out the rusty screws holding the latch. "That did it!" Missy said, as the latch fell to the side and she pushed open the door.

The shed smelled moldy. A dirty wooden counter covered one wall and Missy ran her light over it. Three car radios with wires sprouting from their backs. Four little speakers. Two big speakers. A pile of cassettes. A black leather briefcase. A tin box. A jar of nails and screws. A bashed-in box of slug bait.

"Not much here," I said.

"No. You'd think they'd have a bigger haul." Missy flashed the light on the opposite wall. A rake, a shovel, a crowbar, and an iron chain hung from bent nails.

This was all too creepy for me. "Let's leave before someone comes."

"Wait a minute. I wanna see what's in this box." She put the flashlight down and began prying the lid from the tin box. I stood on one foot and then the other foot, waiting for her to get the top off.

"What's that sound?" Every cell in my body went on alert. "That's a car! That's a car coming up the alley. Let's get out of here."

"Wait! Wait!" She'd grabbed ahold of my shirt.

"They'll see us if we go out the door. It might not be the Dormans. Get under the counter."

I tried to pull away. I wanted over that fence. Missy held on. A car door slammed. Missy grabbed the flashlight, dived under the counter, and I dived after her.

"Who left this door open?" It was Bob's voice and he sounded mad.

"I don't know. I slammed it when we left." That was Derek.

"You dumb jerk. Did you lock it? I told you to lock it."

"I thought I locked it."

I forced my breath in and out slowly and silently while the brothers talked. Missy had squashed herself into the farthest corner under the counter and I huddled against her.

We heard rattling from the doorway. "The screws are out of this thing. You proably knocked them out when you slammed the door."

"I thought I locked it."

Light flooded into the shed.

"Put the stuff down over there," Bob ordered.

Thumps landed on the counter above us. This time they must have brought in a haul. I guess Derek thought so, too, because he said, "The deck should go for thirty bucks and the phones should bring in fifty."

"We better get seventy-five. Those things cost four

hundred new. Hey! What's this hammer doing here? It doesn't look like ours. Did you leave it here?"

I jabbed my elbow into Missy.

"I don't remember leaving any hammer here," Derek said.

"If you didn't, who did?"

"I don't know. Carlson was here last night. Maybe Carlson did."

"Carlson doesn't carry hammers."

Silence. What was Bob thinking? I just hoped and hoped and hoped he didn't look under the counter.

"There'll be big trouble if someone busted in." The threat in Bob's voice stopped my breathing altogether.

"But Wigger was sleeping when we pulled up," Derek said.

"You're right. Let's see what Mom's doing."

There was a scrape from the counter above us. Footsteps to the door. Darkness. A door slam. Rattling and four hard bangs.

I let my breath out. "I bet we're locked in," I whispered. "Now what are we going to do?"

Missy didn't move. I jabbed her again. "How're we going to get out of here?"

"I don't know," she whispered back.

I held perfectly still a minute, listening for sounds outside the shed. "Do you think they're gone?"

"I don't know."

I waited a few more minutes before I wiggled out

from under the counter, crept toward the door, and pushed on it a couple times. "We are locked in. Bob probably used nails to replace the screws."

Missy fumbled toward me. "I guess we'll have to break the window."

"The window faces their house."

"Then I guess we'll have to wait until they leave or they go to bed."

"What will your folks do when they find out we're gone?"

"I don't know. Call your place. Call the police. I don't know."

"You sound like Derek. You—" There was a noise outside. "What's that? Is that car coming or going?"

"It's coming." Missy crept back along the counter with me right behind her. When we got to the end, she ducked under and I scraped my forehead ducking after her.

We could hear a car door slam and then voices. Bob's and a stranger's deeper one.

"Missy!" I hissed. "Missy, as soon as the shed door opens, we rush out of here."

"No, no. They'll grab us."

"But it's our only chance to surprise them. Get down on your hands and knees so we can make a sprint for it."

"No, no. Wait until they leave."

I thought for a couple seconds and decided she could

stay if she wanted, but I'd had enough of following her ideas. So I ignored her whimpers and got on my hands and knees on the grimy wood floor and braced myself for the break. I was going to rush right through Bob and Derek and whoever else was out there. I was going to tear right past them and out the door and—

"Missy," I said, "where's their gate that goes to the alley?"

"Near the shed." She was quivering with fear.

"Where 'near the shed'?"

She didn't answer.

"Where?" I said louder and then clapped my hand over my mouth. The voices outside were coming closer.

"Over to the right about ten fee—" Missy choked at the rattling of the padlock.

Every muscle in my body tensed. I was going to rush by them as soon as the door opened. I was going to—

The door squeaked. The light came on.

"Come on in," Bob said. "We'll show—"

I sprinted out from under the counter and tore by Bob and the other guy. Derek was behind them and he said, "Hey!" and grabbed at my arm. I yanked free of him, went for the fence, and tripped in the dark.

"Sic 'em, Wigger," Derek yelled.

As I scrambled to my knees, I felt Wigger's doggy breath in my face. Terrorized by the vision of his huge jaws clamping on my neck, I lunged for the gate ahead of me. I could see it from the light in the shed.

I barreled through, slammed it shut on Wigger, and ripped down the alley with Missy's screams following me. "Dad-dy! Let me go! Let me go! Daddy! Daaad-dy!"

I made it to Missy's backyard, slipped once in the grass, and then crashed halfway up her steps. The porch light came on and the door flashed open. Mr. Mitchell stared down at me. "*What* is going on?"

"Help Missy. Help Missy." I was panting so hard I could barely get the words out. "Please help Missy. They've got her."

"Where? Where is she?"

"Bob Dorman has her. In his shed."

Mr. Mitchell pounded down the steps, flinging directions behind him, "Get in the house! Call 911!"

He disappeared down the dark alley while I stumbled up to Missy's back door.

12

I'D BARELY hung up the phone and was trying to stutter out answers to Mrs. Mitchell's frantic questions when Missy burst into the house. Her mom rushed across the living room to grab her. "My baby, you're all right!"

Missy managed a nod, even though her face was smashed tight against her mom's chest.

Mrs. Mitchell loosened her grip to stroke Missy's wiry hair over and over. "But where'd your daddy go?"

"He's . . . he's . . . he's hiding in the alley waiting for the cops."

"Oh, my baby, you're in shock." Mrs. Mitchell propelled her over to the couch, sat her down, kneeled in front of her, and peered into her face. "That man—He didn't do anything bad to you, did he?"

Missy shook her head.

I sat on the couch beside her and could feel her trembling. I didn't feel very good myself, but nobody was paying any attention to me. "Did Bob Dorman see your dad?" I asked.

"N-no. I ran into Daddy in the alley. He told me to come home."

Red and blue lights flashed through the living room windows. "The police are here," I said. "Do you think they'll catch the Dormans?"

Missy didn't answer. She just kept on shivering, her pale blue eyes staring at nothing.

"All that matters is that you girls are home," Mrs. Mitchell said. But from the way her fingers drummed against her top lip, I had trouble believing her.

What if Bob Dorman got away? The first time he caught us on the street, he'd pound Missy and me for sure.

Mrs. Mitchell got up to go into the kitchen and look out the door. After she came back, she perched on a chair across from us. "What can your father be doing out there this long?"

How would we know? The lights were still flashing in the windows. Anyway, all I cared about was the cops catching Bob Dorman. "May I use your bath-room?" I asked Mrs. Mitchell.

"Certainly," she said.

It was probably a dumb thing for me to ask since I was supposed to be staying all night.

After I got on the toilet, I pushed my jeans down to check my knees. The left one was scraped, but the right one was bloody from my fall on the steps. I washed it off the best I could with a wad of toilet paper.

When I went back into the living room, Mr. Mitchell was there, trying to calm down his wife. "Now the police are taking care of everything, Arlene. There is nothing more to worry about."

"But what has been happening out there all this time?" she asked.

That's what I wanted to know, too. I sat down on the edge of the couch to listen.

"The police drove up while Derek, Bob, and another man were cleaning out the shed and loading the contents into the Dormans' car," Mr. Mitchell said. "When Derek saw the police, he dropped a cassette deck and tried to run."

"Did they catch him?" I asked.

"Yes, he stopped when the police told him to freeze. They spread him out on the ground and he started crying. I don't think they'll have any trouble getting a confession out of him."

"But what have the Dorman brothers been doing?" Mrs. Mitchell's eyes were squinting with confusion.

I don't think that woman's too swift. She'd heard me explain to 911 what they'd been doing and then she'd asked me the same questions she was asking her husband now.

"Evidently they've been breaking into cars and hiding the contraband in their shed until they could sell it," he explained patiently. "They caught the girls in there. After the girls got away, the Dormans tried to take off with the stolen property as fast as they could."

"But what were the girls doing in the shed?"

Oh, oh. I slid back on the seat cushion and made myself as little as possible.

"That," Mr. Mitchell said, "is a good point."

He pulled a chair up close to the couch and leaned toward Missy. "Just what *were* you doing in the shed?"

"We were just looking at their stuff," Missy said in a little voice.

Mr. Mitchell frowned. "How did you get over there? Why would you be over there in the night?"

"We just—" Missy shrugged her shoulders helplessly.

Mr. Mitchell turned to me. "Caitlin, will you please tell me clearly what you and Missy did this evening."

"Well," I started out. "Umm. We ordered pizza. And we looked at the movie. And then we usually play with Wigger, the dog next door. And . . . Did the police catch Bob Dorman?"

"They have the license number and the description of the man's car who was with the Dormans. He and Bob jumped in that car when the police arrived. They expect to pick them up tonight."

"But Bob got away?"

"Temporarily. Now, what were you girls doing in their shed?"

I slunk even further into the couch cushions, trying desperately to think of an excuse to go home.

"Can one of you girls answer me?" Mr. Mitchell's voice was getting sharp.

"I'm scared of Bob Dorman," Missy mumbled.

"Well, he isn't going to hurt you here. *How* did you get in the neighbor's yard?"

"We climbed over the fence." She said this so softly, even I could barely hear her.

"And why did you climb over the fence?" he demanded. "And don't tell me it was to play with the dog."

So much for my feeble excuses.

Missy took a sideways glance at me and must have figured I wasn't going to be any more help. She focused on Mr. Mitchell's glasses, obviously trying to get it together. "Well, when I tell you things, Daddy, you never believe me. And . . . and we thought the Dormans were stealing things and maybe we should just peek in their shed to see what they were hiding before we told anyone. Because you always say I imagine things."

That didn't go over.

Mr. Mitchell measured each word. "And what made you think the Dormans were stealing?"

"We heard them talking. Bob Dorman was mad at Derek for trying to steal a tape deck out of a Mercedes. Bob was yelling at Derek because those cars have alarms." About this time, even Missy could see her story wasn't making it with her dad. She added feebly, "They were yelling so loud next door, we couldn't help hearing them."

"And so you decided to play girl detective. How old are you?"

"I'm twelve."

"Twelve, eh? When you were four years old, I didn't expect you to weigh the consequences of your acts. Now it's eight years later and you're still as heedless as when you were four."

"But, Daddy—"

"How," Mr. Mitchell interrupted her, "did you get into the shed?"

"We . . . uh . . . we pulled out the screws holding the padlock. They were . . . they were rusty."

"What did you use to pull them out?"

Oh, boy, I thought, she's trapped now.

Missy blinked her eyes and shot a glance at her

mother before she answered. "Umm . . . uh . . . we . . . borrowed your hammer."

"And where is my hammer now?" Mr. Mitchell's deadly tone scared me even worse then Bob Dorman's had. I wanted to go home.

"I don't know," she said. A big tear rolled down her cheek.

This upset her mom, but her dad's expression remained stony cold. He leaned even farther toward Missy and pointed a long finger at her chest. "You had better not behave in such a stupid and dangerous manner ever again. And to see that you don't—"

Mrs. Mitchell jumped to her feet. "Dear, Missy's had a frightening experience tonight. I think that will be a sufficient lesson for her."

Mr. Mitchell turned around to look at his wife. "Oh, you do? All right. You're the one who wanted her. She's all yours." He got up from his chair and walked out of the room.

Missy threw her hands over her mouth as if she'd been slapped. Mrs. Mitchell took a step forward. She didn't seem to know whether to go after her husband or go to Missy. I sat there feeling sick. What if my dad gave up on me?

"I think I should go home," I said in a voice that was as little as Missy's had been.

Mrs. Mitchell looked at her watch. "It's almost twelve o'clock. Your parents are probably asleep. Why don't you and Missy go on to bed. We'll take you home after breakfast."

"Okay," I agreed, but I wasn't very happy about it.

Missy didn't have much to say while we put on our pajamas. I did ask her a couple of questions after we'd gotten into bed. "How did you get away from Bob Dorman anyway?"

"I bit him," she said. "He had his hand over my mouth to make me stop screaming and I bit his finger so hard my teeth hit the bone. When he yanked his hand away and hauled off to hit me, I ran."

"What did Derek and the other guy do?"

"I was running as fast as I could and all I could hear was Derek hollering, 'Sic 'em, Wigger. Sic 'em.' "

I know the whole thing wasn't funny. But the picture of dumb Derek thinking that fat Wigger would attack Missy, after all the roast and cheese she'd fed him, started me giggling. I just couldn't help myself.

"I was really scared, Caitlin. That Bob Dorman's mean."

"I know. I'm sorry." I turned over and stuffed the pillow against my face to muffle my giggles.

———

I WOKE up and looked out the window at the morning sun turning the water from the sprinkler into loops of diamonds. Missy snuffled beside me, still sound asleep. I arched my body into a long stretch.

115

Then, remembering, I yanked my knees up to my stomach. Bob Dorman. Had the police caught Bob Dorman yet?

I listened for sounds in the house. I thought I heard someone walking from the kitchen to the living room. I hoped it was Mrs. Mitchell. I didn't want to see Mr. Mitchell again. Especially not Mr. Mitchell with Missy.

I eased out of bed, trotted to the bathroom and back, and pulled on my clothes. Mrs. Mitchell had said she'd take me home. It was too scary to go by myself.

I thought I was slipping quietly into the living room, but as soon as I got through the door, Mr. Mitchell looked up from his paper.

"Hi," I said.

"Good morning," he said. "Are you ready for some breakfast?"

"No, thank you. I think I'd better go home." I eased a little farther into the room. "Did they catch Bob Dorman yet?"

"Not that I've heard. I was going to wait until eight o'clock before I checked with the police."

"Oh." I shifted from one foot to the other, not knowing if it would be worse to ask him for a ride or try to race down the block and a half alone.

Mr. Mitchell was watching me intently. I'd noticed when he did pay attention to someone he looked right into their eyes. "Would you like me to drive you to your house?" he asked.

"I guess so," I said.

He didn't say anything and I didn't say anything during the short ride. As he pulled up in front of my house, I gathered my tote bag into my lap.

"Perhaps I'd better come in and explain to your parents about last night," he suggested.

I put my hand on the door handle. "What time is it?"

"About six-thirty."

"Oh, I don't think my mom will be up yet." I pushed down the handle and hopped out.

"Caitlin!" he called out his window as I rounded the front of the car. "After I talk to the police, I'll call your parents."

"My dad's on the road."

"I'll speak to your mother then."

"Thank you very much for the ride," I said politely and ran up the steps to my door.

13

I PACED my room and practiced my speech, impatiently waiting for Mom to wake up. There was nothing else to do. Even Jimmy was sound asleep. Each fifteen minutes added to my worry that Mr. Mitchell would call before I could talk to Mom.

In my house, you're in half as much trouble if you tell on yourself as you are if someone tells on you. I was about to take a chance on making Mom grumpy by waking her up, when I heard the downstairs toilet flush. I bolted out of my room.

In the kitchen, I decided it would look too phony if I heated water for her coffee. I just made a jug of frozen orange juice and casually put two glasses and two napkins out on the table.

"You're home early," she said when she came in.

"Umm, ya. There was a little excitement over at the Mitchells' house."

Mom raised her eyebrows. "Excitement? And you left?"

"I'll tell you all about it while you're eating. Want some orange juice?"

"Yes, thank you. But first I want to get my coffee started."

I sat down on a chair and tried not to look jumpy. If the phone didn't ring and Jimmy didn't cry, I could get my story told. If either made a peep, I was dead.

"Now," Mom said, after she'd put her cup of water in the microwave and joined me at the table, "what was all the excitement about?"

"Well, you know the Dormans live next door to Missy and they have this big bulldog?"

Mom nodded and took a sip of orange juice.

"Well, Missy made friends with him and sometimes we played with him in the backyard. Well, we heard Bob and Derek talking and it sounded like they were breaking into cars. Stealing radios and cassettes out of them and hiding the stuff in their shed."

"You heard all this?" Mom asked. "When?"

"While we were out in back. Bob was mad at Derek for almost getting them caught and so he was doing a lot of yelling." I thought it was best to rush over how much time had gone by. Otherwise, I might get tangled up explaining why we hadn't let her or Mr. Mitchell know about the Dormans.

"Anyway, Missy and I decided to look in their shed to see if they'd really stolen anything. So we climbed over the fence to peek in their shed—"

Mom put her glass down with a thump. "Caitlin, that was a sneaky thing to do. Why didn't you tell the Mitchells what you heard?"

"Oh, they were gone. Remember I told you they keep their clinic open until nine on Fridays? I know it was dumb of us to go over there, but the Dorman brothers had left and we were just going to take a little look." I could hear squeaks from upstairs and knew Jimmy was awake, but Mom had all her attention on me, so I rushed on.

"But while we were looking in the shed, the Dorman brothers came back and caught us. I got away first and ran to Missy's house, and the Mitchells were home by then and Mr. Mitchell told me to call 911 and he went to get Missy, but she'd already gotten away from Bob Dorman. And then the cops came and arrested Derek Dorman, but they didn't catch Bob."

Mom was staring at me as if she were having trouble

120

believing all this. Jimmy was crooning upstairs. He'd probably filled his pants.

"Caitlin," Mom said. "The police wouldn't come without a warrant to search the shed."

"Oh. Well, you see, I reported that Bob had Missy and she was only twelve. And then the Dorman brothers and another man were trying to get all their stuff out of the shed and into Bob's car when the cops came, so they caught Derek red-handed. Only Bob and the other guy got away in the other guy's car. Mr. Mitchell is going to call you today when he finds out if the police captured Bob yet."

Right then the phone rang. That was fine with me because, from the glints in Mom's eyes, I knew she was getting ready to give me a real grilling.

"You take care of the baby," she said. "I'll get the phone."

Jimmy was a mess, of course. While I changed his stinky diapers and swabbed him down, I tried to listen to the conversation downstairs. All I could hear were mumbles. Jimmy thinks it's funny to kick his feet while you're trying to put on his overalls. By the time I got him dressed and down in the living room, Mom was about ready to hang up.

"Thank you very much for calling and I'll appreciate your letting me know when Bob Dorman is in custody."

Ugh. They didn't have him yet.

121

"Yes, I agree with you," Mom went on. "This really isn't like Caitlin at all. She's usually a responsible girl. But I will completely support you."

Oh, oh. This was some kind of punishment, I knew. I lugged Jimmy into the kitchen to poke cereal down him before I gave him his bottle.

Mom followed me in. "I just can't understand you, Caitlin. Mr. Mitchell said you broke into the shed."

"It was no big thing, Mom. The screws were all rusty. Missy just pulled them out."

"It is too a big thing. You went into someone's yard and broke into their shed. And do you have any idea the danger you put yourself in? And are still in? It's lucky you and Missy weren't hurt." Mom's eyes closed as she dropped into her chair.

I concentrated on Jimmy. He was turning his head every time I brought the spoon close to his mouth. That meant he'd had enough. I wiped his face, took off his bib, and handed him to Mom. "Here, hold him while I warm his milk."

Jimmy patted Mom's cheek and that got a little smile out of her. I grabbed the chance to change the subject. "I don't want to go to school Monday if they haven't caught Bob Dorman. I'm afraid of him."

"Then why didn't you think before you climbed over his fence?"

There was no answer to that. After Jimmy's bottle

was warm, I gave it to her. He was still patting her cheek and cooing to her and she couldn't keep the frown on her face. That kid is definitely on my side.

When Jimmy had a good grip on the bottle and was sucking away in Mom's lap, she turned her attention back on me. "I don't want you over at Missy's again unless her parents are home. And they don't want you over there, either."

"You mean it's all my fault?"

"No. Nobody's saying it's all your fault. But you are responsible for what you do. And lately you've been following that girl around like she was the mother duck. That girl is far too harem-scarem for my comfort. You find yourself someone else to play with."

"Who? Bones?"

"I don't know 'who.' Here, take Jimmy out in the sun and let me have some breakfast."

I picked Jimmy up from her lap, went out the door, and plopped him onto the grass under the apple tree. He'd kept a death grip on his bottle the whole way. I sat down beside him, thinking that so far I'd gotten off pretty easy. You can't tell about my mom, though. She might stew over the break-in and decide I needed a stiffer punishment.

I'm not sure how Bones does it, but he always seems to know when I'm out in the yard. Maybe he listens for my back door to close, like I listen for his. Jimmy didn't have his bottle half-finished before Bones came through the gate.

He crouched down a couple yards from me and started plucking grass blades from the ground and running them through his teeth. Bones never moves very close to anybody and he never visits without a reason. I fiddled with Jimmy's fat little toes and let Bones do the talking for a change.

All he had on were khaki shorts, and the hot morning sun piercing through the apple branches made bright patches on his tanned skin. A thin layer of flesh covered his bones and he no longer looked like a skeleton. A hunk, I thought to myself. He was slowly turning into a hunk.

He shot me a quick glance. "You see the cops over by your friend's house last night?"

"Sure, how come you saw them?"

"They had their light show on for a half hour. You could see it for blocks."

"I saw their lights flashing from Missy's living room window." That's all I said. And then waited, enjoying every second.

"So?" He raised an eyebrow.

"So, they were after the Dormans."

"Why?"

"Because Missy and I sicced them on them."

Bones's dark gray eyes grew darker. "How come?"

It was then I remembered Bones talking to Bob Dorman. And the digging in the night. The trouble with Missy had shoved it from my mind.

"How come?" Bones repeated.

There was a steely tone to his voice that made me decide to stop being cute and tell him what really happened. I started out by reminding him that Missy and I had made friends with Wigger.

"Ya, and so?" Bones said.

"Well, so we could go in their yard."

He gave me a look that let me know he thought I was crazy.

"*Because*, Bones, we heard Bob and Derek talk about ripping off cars."

Bones ducked his head and spit out some of the grass he had in his mouth. I waited for him to look back up at me, but he didn't. I went ahead and told him about getting caught in the shed and Mr. Mitchell telling me to dial 911, and the police catching Derek but not Bob Dorman. "And Mr. Mitchell called my mom today and the police still haven't got Bob."

Bones slowly stood up. "You'd better stay in your yard until they do," he said and left, slamming the garden gate after himself.

Jimmy had dropped his empty bottle, rolled over on his stomach, and urped up a blob of milk. I gave his back an extra rub before I lifted him into my arms. As I turned to go in the house, I saw Mrs. Kager puttering around in her backyard. She'd probably heard Bones and my whole conversation.

In the living room, Mom was talking to a client on the phone. When she finished, she called Susan, told her about the Dormans, and asked her to spend the morning at our house. "Now listen to me," Mom said after she hung up. "I have to be gone for two hours. Susan is coming over to stay with you. *Do not* leave the house. *Do not* open the door."

"You sound like the Nanny Goat," I said.

"This isn't funny, Caitlin. You take care of Jimmy and put him down for his nap. Susan's going to bring her book-work with her."

Mom went in her room to put on her business suit. I sat on the floor with Jimmy and bounced a red ball in front of him. He snatched at it until he caught it in his hand.

Susan hadn't arrived by the time Mom was ready to leave. Mom tried to call her again, but there was no answer. "Go ahead and leave," I said. "We'll be safe until she gets here."

Mom looked at her watch. "Susan *must* be on her way." She checked her watch again, then bent down and lifted my chin. "*You* stay in the house."

"I will."

Jimmy dropped the ball and held up his arms. Mom blew him a kiss before she hurried out the door. I locked it behind her.

126

I love Jimmy, but babies get boring after you play with them a half hour. I knew that was how much time had gone by because I checked the kitchen clock. Just when I returned to the living room, I heard someone pound across the front porch. He came with heavy steps, not Susan's light steps.

I stood still, feeling my heart race in my chest and my face go hot.

Two hard knocks on the door.

If I don't move, he will go away, I thought. He will think no one's home and go away.

I didn't make a move, but Jimmy swatted his ball and when it rolled, he let out a squeal.

I clamped my teeth over the fingers I'd shoved in my mouth. Should I grab Jimmy and run for my room?

Two more knocks, louder now.

I grabbed for Jimmy, but the knocks had scared him and he screamed and slithered out of my arms. "Come on!" I whispered desperately and caught him by his leg.

"U.P.S.!" the man called out.

I let go of Jimmy and crept to the window, my heart still racing. I carefully pulled the drape aside. It *was* the U.P.S. man.

"I'm sorry. I didn't know it was you," I told him after I'd unlocked the door.

He poked his clipboard at me. "Please sign here."

I signed and took the package. It was for Mom, from Dad.

Susan drove up as the U.P.S. truck pulled out. I held the door open for her. "What kept you?"

"You'll never guess." She took off her coat and flopped on the couch. "I was hurrying to get here and I got a ticket for going fifty in a thirty-five mile zone."

"Oh, no!"

"Oh, yes! Now sit down and tell me your cops and robbers story."

It was fun telling Susan because she's young enough not to think everything I do is dumb. We were drinking Cokes together when Mom came home. Dad's package turned out to be a box of chocolates for their anniversary.

That put Mom in a good mood. Around about Jimmy's bedtime, though, I noticed her frowning in thought. The magazine she had been reading was lying in her lap.

"Jimmy hasn't had a bath today," I said. "I'll put him in the tub with me."

She hesitated before she agreed. My mom's a little lazy about household things. I knew she didn't want to get out of her chair to be soaked by Jimmy slipping around in his Bathinette. But I also guessed she was about ready to tackle me and the shed once more. Her laziness won.

I brought him downstairs, pink and shiny clean in

his sleepers. He patted Mom's cheek again when I tipped him to her for a kiss. That made her laugh. Jimmy was gradually weaseling himself into Mom's heart.

"I'll say goodnight, too. I've got a pile of homework to do before I go to bed." I pecked her on the mouth and hurried Jimmy and me back up the stairs.

I didn't do any homework, of course. Instead, I stretched out on my covers and thought about Bones. He hadn't asked any questions about what was in the shed.

I was almost positive he already knew. But why did he get upset over the Dormans being busted? Why would Bones care if they got caught? And what had he been talking to Bob Dorman about?

I fell asleep with the light on and had an ugly nightmare. I was running and running as fast as I could up a long, long, pitch-black alley. The sounds of Bob's feet were pounding behind me. Just as I felt him grab me by my hair, I woke up covered with sweat.

I got off the bed and brushed my teeth and washed my face. In the mirror I said to myself, "Please, please catch that Bob Dorman."

I'd switched off my lamp and had almost fallen asleep again when I heard the *scritch, scritch, scritch* of a shovel cutting through dirt. Dig away, I thought. I don't care.

I wasn't going out on the deck to see who it was.

I'd never told Mom about the midnight digging and if she caught me snooping again, even Jimmy couldn't save me. I turned over, punched my pillow into a hollow for my chin, and closed my eyes.

They flew open again at the tell-tale squeak of the Reddings' basement door. Somebody was watching somebody out there.

14

SUNDAY morning, I decided to tell Mom about the digging so I'd have everything off my conscience. I waited until she'd downed half her breakfast before I started my story. "You know," I said, "there's something funny about the Reddings."

Three light taps hit our kitchen door.

"Speak of the devil." Mom got up to let Mrs. Redding in.

"Oh, Karen," Mrs. Redding said, "I hope I'm not interrupting anything."

"No," Mom said, "I don't have an appointment

until ten-thirty." Once in a while, Mom has appointments on Sunday morning. This time I wasn't sure if she had one or just wanted to make certain she could get rid of Mrs. Redding in an hour.

Mom got a mug out of the cupboard, filled it with water, and shoved it in the microwave. There was no point in asking Mrs. Redding if she'd like some coffee. She always did.

After Mrs. Redding was settled at the table with the coffee and she'd helped herself to two spoonfuls of sugar, she stretched her neck toward Mom. "Did you know a patrol car was stationed in the alley behind the Dormans' house on Friday night?"

"I'd heard about it," Mom said.

Since I'd heard about it, too, I left the room to get Jimmy up. He was better company.

Forty-five minutes later, when I brought Jimmy into the kitchen to feed him his cereal, the conversation had moved on to Mrs. Reddings' favorite subject, money. "I think Paul will have to work this summer to help out," she was saying.

"But," Mom objected, "he isn't fourteen yet, is he?"

"He will be in July. He can pick berries until he's old enough to get a work permit."

Bones would love that, I thought. He'd love crawling on the ground in the blistering sun.

Mom shook her head. "Edith, I don't understand how you can be so hard up. Your house insurance paid

132

off your mortgage when your husband died and you get Social Security payments for Paul, don't you?"

"Yes, but I only get them until Paul's eighteen. What will I do after that? There's inflation and what if my taxes go up again?"

"Your salary will go up, too," Mom said.

"Maybe not." Mrs. Redding looked as if a ghost were on her tail. "Maybe I'll be too old and they'll fire me."

"That's a foolish worry, Edith. You work in a nursing home. But if you want to feel more secure, why don't you call the hospitals and clinics around here and see if you can pick up some weekend work. You could start a savings account with the extra money."

Mrs. Redding's eyelids shriveled into slits. "I don't trust banks. They can fail."

Mom sighed, obviously giving up. So much for Bones's summer.

I had my chin clamped over Jimmy's head to keep him from squirming on my lap. It took two hands to tie his bib.

Mom noticed. "For heaven's sake, Caitlin, let me help you. You'll have his vertebrae squashed before he's old enough to go to a chiropractor."

I lifted Jimmy up by his arms and dangled him in front of Mom while she tied his bib. I could feel irritation oozing out of her. Mrs. Redding's visits do that.

"I guess I'd better be getting on home, Karen. You'll want to get ready for your appointment." Mrs. Redding picked up her mug and spoon, put them in the sink, and moved slowly toward the door.

When she'd gotten herself outside, I said, "Maybe she should find a new husband."

Mom didn't bother to comment on that. "I have to make a callback on an old couple. Get Jimmy's sweater and ride along with me."

"Okay," I agreed. She wanted us along because of Bob Dorman, I knew. Nutty Mrs. Redding had made me forget him for a few minutes.

When Mom stopped our car at her customer's house, I climbed in the front seat with Jimmy and locked all the doors. Mom stayed inside the house for an hour. All the time I was amusing Jimmy by turning his toes into little piggies and his fingers into spider legs, I wished I'd called Missy to see if Mr. Mitchell had heard from the police. But then I kept remembering Mom saying, "And they don't want you over there, either."

This made me half-hurt and half-mad. Even though Missy kept repeating what *we* did, in answer to her dad's questions, none of it had been my idea. Missy's a lot braver getting into things than she is getting out of them. I decided I'd bring that up the next time I didn't want to go along with her.

Jimmy fell asleep before Mom came out of the

house. I turned on some music and was tapping on the steering wheel while absentmindedly watching a car with big rear tires park down the block. It was built like Bob Dorman's car, which always looks like it's lifting its hind end to squat. I didn't really think it was Bob's car, but I stopped tapping to the music until I saw the bald-headed driver.

Mom startled me by knocking on the window. I unlocked the door and got out for her. She was in a good mood because she'd made a double sale.

She chattered away while I got in the back and she stashed her briefcase on the floor below Jimmy's car seat. "And I'm positive both the man and his wife will qualify. The woman has diabetes, but she isn't taking insulin, so she should get accepted."

As if I cared.

Mom looked down at her suit before she put her key in the ignition. "I think I'll get a light jacket for summer. Caitlin, how would you like some new shorts?"

I did care!

We woke up Jimmy when we reached the Alderwood Mall. Mom got a linen jacket, I got shorts and a top, Jimmy got a Mariners cap. Mom and I porked out on "All You Can Eat" at Skippers while Jimmy slurped up his bottle of apple juice.

On the way home, he twisted around in his car seat to look at me while he clawed his hands in the air.

"What a smart kid," I said to Mom. "He remembers the song."

She tilted her head his way with a smile and for the rest of the ride, we sang the "Itsy Bitsy Spider" to him.

The phone was ringing as we came up our front steps. Mom got the door open in time to answer it. I could tell it was Mr. Mitchell by the formal way she talked.

"I'm sure Caitlin will be glad to hear this," she said into the receiver. "We've been concerned about her attending school tomorrow. Thank you very much for calling."

They'd caught Bob Dorman! I collapsed onto the davenport in relief.

———◆———

BONES didn't have much to say on the way to school in the morning. Even after I told him the police had Bob Dorman, his eyes just narrowed a bit. I was feeling pretty good in my new shorts. And I wanted to chatter to him about the digging and his sack of clothes and what he'd talked to Bob about. The words "Reach out and touch someone," flitted through my mind. But you can't touch Bones.

He left me at the corner to go down to the gas station. I crossed over to Missy's side of the street, but I walked right past her house.

"Why didn't you stop for me?" she asked when she caught up. "Is it because of what Daddy said? He's still ignoring me. What did your mom do?"

"Nothing."

"Didn't she ground you or anything?"

"No."

"I wish I weren't adopted."

"What's that got to do with it?" I was thinking I really didn't like Missy much.

"You wouldn't know," Missy whined. "It's terrible being adopted."

"My sister Susan's adopted. And Mom likes to be with her more than me. They have more in common."

"But you're not adopted."

"No, Mom thought she couldn't have any kids when she took Susan. Then nine years later, she had me, and eleven years later, she had Jimmy. She was real mad about being pregnant with him." Letting that out made me feel disloyal. I added, "But she's getting used to him now."

"Well, I haven't got anything in common with my dad."

I did with mine, but I didn't think I should rub it in. Missy's face was lumpy with misery, and her tight black skirt made her stomach look fat. I smiled down at my new apple-green shorts.

"You know that boy you're always following around," Missy said suddenly.

"You mean my neighbor, Paul."

Missy wrinkled her face. "You called him Bones."

"Okay, Bones. What about him?"

"Well, guys are still cruising the alley looking for Bob and Derek. And your Bones was out there last night. I saw him leaning into one car window for a long time. Maybe he steals, too."

"No, Bones doesn't! Anyway, shut up. Here comes Arthur." Arthur was halfway down his steps and I didn't want Missy spreading that story around.

As we passed his house, Arthur turned in behind us and walked on our heels just like he always does. "Say, what were the cops doing at your house Friday night?" he asked Missy.

"They were next door at the Dormans' because I found out they were thieves." Missy went on to tell Arthur the whole story. I noticed this time she dropped the *we's* and barely mentioned that I'd been along. I didn't bother correcting her. I was too worried about Bones. What was he doing in the alley?

Jill, Lindsi, and Robert were standing on the parking strip in front of the school when we arrived. I checked across the street to see if Bones was at the junior high yet. He wasn't.

"Cute shorts!" Jill said.

"I saw some like those at Nordstroms," Lindsi said. "Only my mom wouldn't get them because her credit card was over the limit."

Robert had opened his spelling book and was standing there mouthing the words to himself. "You're a student now?" I said.

"My dad's going to buy me a new mitt if I get an A on this test."

"Nooo!" I screeched. "I forgot all about the test. I even left my book at home."

"You can't borrow mine," Arthur told me in his piggy, prissy way.

"Who wants to," I said.

The bell rang and we all moved toward the school doors while I desperately tried to figure out how I was going to pass the test.

After roll call, Mrs. Shivelly led a discussion on who should represent our class on a tour of the junior high. "When the school was smaller," she said, "the whole sixth grade class visited the junior high in the spring. Now we're so large, we can have only four representatives from each sixth grade room.

"I'll take nominations from you today and then we can have the vote on Friday. That will give you time to think over who will be able to ask intelligent questions about the junior high curriculum and bring you answers that will be helpful to you in planning your schedule for next year."

"Can we nominate ourselves?" Arthur asked.

"Certainly," Mrs. Shivelly said.

Arthur nominated himself. Jill nominated Lindsi.

Lindsi nominated Jill. Jaime nominated Robert. Lee nominated Stephanie.

It didn't make any difference to me who got elected. Jill had passed me her spelling book and I had it open in my lap, studying the words like mad.

We had the test just before lunch. I remembered some of the words. Except *concept.* How do you spell *concept?* With a *c* or an *s?*

Arthur was practically lying on his paper so I couldn't see it. I left a blank space in the word and went onto the next one Mrs. Shivelly pronounced. When the finished papers were passed forward, I took a quick peek and then wrote in a *c* on mine. Arthur watched me with a disgusted look on his face.

That night I worried some more about Bones before I went to sleep. Missy's so nosy that if Bones were up to something, she might find out. And what was *her* dad doing with a loose car phone? Maybe he liked Bob Dorman's discounts.

Thinking about dads made me wonder if that was what Bones needed. My dad has a cool head. He was coming home on Saturday. I promised myself I'd tell him about the digging and Bob and the alley. Maybe he could figure out what was going on before something bad happened to Bones.

15

MISSY was crabby all week. Bones was silent. I wished he would talk to me, but I didn't care much about Missy. I'd expected her to hold court at recess, telling all the kids how *she* had caught Bob Dorman. She didn't. She was still smarting over her dad's crossing her off.

"Why don't you apologize to him?" I asked her on the way to school Friday morning.

"It wouldn't do any good," she said. "He doesn't like me anymore."

"Sure he does. My mom says she might not like what *I do*, but she always loves *me*."

"You're not adopted."

"That doesn't make any difference. I asked my mom and she said she'd never give up on Susan any more than she would on me or Jimmy."

Missy hardly listened to what I said. She has a one-track mind.

When we got to Arthur's house, he came down the steps wearing a computer-printed label on his shirt. "What does that say?" I asked.

He poked his chest toward us. The sign read JUNIOR HIGH REP.

"What makes you think you're going to get elected?" I wanted to know.

"Because there were only five people nominated and four get elected. Maybe I'm not the most popular kid in the room, but I'm the smartest. Robert couldn't report anything correctly. Who's going to vote for him?"

"Half the class," I said. "Your logic only works on computers."

"We'll see," he said.

We saw. The voting took place just before lunch. Mrs. Shively read off the five names from the blackboard, told us to vote intelligently, and asked us to put our heads down. Arthur shot me his know-it-all smirk before he dropped his head on his arms.

I raised my hand for Lindsi. I like Jill best, but Lindsi always has it together and would make us look good at the junior high. When Mrs. Shivelly said we could bring our heads up, she was erasing the voting numbers and Arthur's name.

"Congratulations to Lindsi, Jill, Robert, and Stephanie." Mrs. Shivelly smiled at each of them. "I'm sure you'll do a good job for the class and make the transition into junior high easier for everyone. Now please clear your desks for lunch."

The two that had been beside Arthur's name was still visible under the smear of powdered chalk. He'd vote for himself, I knew, but who else in the room would? I sneaked a look at him.

He was staring at the blackboard, his eyes glassy with shock. His right hand was crawling up his chest to tear the rep label off his shirt. I guess he really hadn't known the consequences of being a pig.

"I have to turn some statistics into the office this afternoon," Mrs. Shivelly said. "I'd appreciate it if you'd eat your lunches quietly at your own desks today so I can work at mine. The lunch buyers may line up now."

Mom had given me money for lunch. I marched down the hall to the hot lunch carts with the other buyers to get spaghetti, celery sticks, and chocolate pudding.

I tried to eat without looking at Arthur again. And

143

I tried not to feel sorry for him. But when he pushed his lunch sack to the back of the desk and laid his head down, I said, "Arthur, you should have expected that."

"Why?" he asked in a sad voice.

"Because you're conceited and you're selfish." I should have stopped there, but I was trying to straighten him out. "You can't expect kids to vote for you when you've been ramming your brains down their throats all year. You always have to know more than anybody else. And you never want anybody to beat you in a test. You never share anything."

Arthur's head came up slowly. "I spend an hour learning spelling words and you lose your book and want to copy my test."

"I didn't lose my book. I left it home. And I didn't copy your test."

"No, you copied somebody else's."

I shrugged. "So I'm not smart like you."

He squinted his eyes in his mean little way. "You're smart enough. You're just lazy. I've seen the books you read. They're all high-school books. Like that *Time* book you had. That's a high-school book."

"So what? I got it at the public library. I've read all the books in this library."

"All you do is read books. You're too lazy to study. You just mess around with your assignments awhile and then cheat so you'll pass."

"All right, I'm lazy. At least the kids like me."

"Maybe if the kids knew you were a cheater, they'd hate you like you hate your lazy babysitter. People don't like *cheaters!*" Arthur spit out the last word.

The kids were turning their heads to stare at us. Mrs. Shivelly rose from her desk. I watched her out of the corner of my eye until she came to stand in front of our desk. "I thought I asked you students to eat quietly. *What* is this argument about?"

I swallowed twice, panicking over what Arthur would say.

"I'm sorry we disturbed you, Mrs. Shivelly," Arthur said. "I won't talk again."

"Me either," I mumbled.

"Please see that you don't." Mrs. Shivelly returned to her desk.

When school was over, Arthur carefully packed up his textbooks. I did, too. I wanted to thank him for not squealing on me, but I didn't know how to begin. He marched out of the room without once looking my way.

———

SATURDAY afternoon, Mom went to the airport to pick up Dad. Susan came over to take care of Jimmy. I curled up on the davenport to read a book called *In the Mouth of the Wolf*, which is about a Jewish girl working for a German SS Colonel during World War

II. When the phone rang, I picked up the receiver, keeping a finger on my page in the book.

"Hi," Missy said. "Do you want to come over?"

"Your dad's not mad at you anymore?"

"He made breakfast for Mom and me this morning. They're at the clinic now doing their state taxes. So come on over."

"Wait a minute. Your dad said he didn't want me in your house when he wasn't there."

"It doesn't matter because they're gone."

"You're crazy. I'm not going where I'm not wanted. See you Monday." I hung up, thinking that Missy would never change.

The word *change* echoed in my mind as I opened my book again. I'll do my homework as soon as I finish the story, I promised myself. Jill and some of the other kids could have heard Arthur call me a cheater. If I cheated again, they'd know he was telling the truth. And I already felt icky enough about Arthur and what he thought of me.

Mom brought Chinese food home for dinner. She and Susan both had sold five insurance policies during the week and were climbing all over Dad to tell him the details of each sale. About eight o'clock, it became obvious I wasn't going to get him alone to discuss Bones. I went upstairs to read.

I finished my book about nine-thirty and started on

my social studies. It was unbelievably boring. *In the Mouth of the Wolf* is a true story. I don't understand why they can't make school history books interesting.

My mind kept wandering off to Bones. He was getting the money for his new clothes somewhere. But where? And what was he doing in that alley?

Dad came up to take a peek at Jimmy and to kiss me goodnight. For a minute, I thought I had my chance to share my worries about Bones. But before I could even start, Susan called up the stairs to say Dad was wanted on the phone. After he left, I forced myself back to my social studies.

It must have been about an hour later that I turned off my light. I had almost floated into sleep when a terrible scream ripped through the night and sat me straight up in bed. It was followed by insane screeching and pleading. "No! Wait! No!"

I tore out of my bed, through the French doors, and onto the deck. In the light of the moon, I saw two figures struggling by the fence. A shovel slashed between them. It was Bones's voice pleading, "Please wait. No!"

I raced back across the deck, through my room, and down the stairs, screaming for help. Dad caught up with me in the kitchen and held me by my shoulders. "What is it, Caitlin?"

"Bones. Somebody's beating Bones."

Dad dropped his hold on me.

"Be careful, Caitlin," Mom said behind me as we followed him out the door.

Dad swore at the latch on the garden gate, but it only stopped him for a second. The awful screeching was going on and on.

When we were halfway across the Reddings' yard, I could see through the dark that it was Mrs. Redding slashing at Bones. Dad yanked the shovel out of her hands. Mom grabbed at her nightgown and tried to hold her. But Mrs. Redding was crazy mad and ripped away to claw at Bones.

Dad dropped the shovel, snatched Mrs. Redding's arms, and pinned them behind her. Bones stood in front of them, panting. I could see a thick line of blood running down his face from a gash on his forehead. He smeared it away with the back of his hand.

Mrs. Redding's screeches dropped to sobs as Dad held her fast. "He's st-stealing from m-me."

"Come on," Dad said. "We'll settle this in our house." He steered Mrs. Redding across her lawn.

Mom caught up with them as they reached our back door, circled an arm around Mrs. Redding's waist, and led her to a kitchen chair. Dad turned on the light. Bones and I stayed by the door. I had no idea what to do.

"Sit down," Dad told us. And to Mom he said, "Why don't you make some coffee."

When Mom put a cup in her hands, Mrs. Redding was shaking so hard she could barely hold it. Bones sat silently at the end of the table, red blood oozing down his chalk white face.

"Edith, tell us what this was all about," Dad said.

"Just a minute," Mom interrupted. "I think we better do something about that cut." She got a box of Band-Aids from the cupboard and wet a paper towel under the faucet.

Bones tipped up his head to let her wash away the blood before she pulled the gash together with the adhesive ends of three Band-Aids. When she was finished, she sat down next to Dad.

He nodded to Mrs. Redding. "Now, can you explain what this is all about?"

"My son is stealing from me."

Dad turned to Bones. "Is this true?"

"I dug up a coin she buried," Bones said.

"A coin! A coin! That was a gold piece worth hundreds of dollars." Mrs. Redding's gray hair poked wildly out from her head. Her eyes looked even wilder. I was afraid she'd go off her rocker again.

Mom spoke sharply. "Edith, take another drink of your coffee."

Dad waited patiently until she'd had several sips. "Tell us," he said, "how many gold coins you have buried."

"I don't know. I'm not sure. I used to keep them in

a strongbox in the basement, but I was afraid someone would break in. So I put them in a jar and buried them. And then I buried two more in small cans after I bought each one." She gave out a little cry. "I thought they'd be safe in the ground."

Mom leaned forward. "But, Edith, where do you get the money?"

"I buy them with the Social Security checks."

"But those checks are for Paul's support. It's illegal to use them for anything else." Mom was frowning.

Dad looked even more stern. "If the Social Security Administration finds out how you've been spending the checks they've sent for Paul, you're in big trouble, lady."

Mrs. Redding shook her head, making her hair fly from side to side. "No, no. No, no. I deposit the checks. I just don't use them until I buy the gold. I buy everything for the house from my wages. Paul hasn't ever needed the extra money. I've always seen that he has everything he needs."

I couldn't believe it. I could not believe she'd say that. But she did. And she said it again.

"I've always taken care of him. And now he—"

"No, you haven't!" I said in a loud voice. "You haven't bought him clothes for years and you've starved him."

"That isn't true." Mrs. Redding huddled back in her

chair, her head still shaking. "We've always had food on the table."

"Sure," I said. "Blue milk that you water down for a week. Why do you think we all call him *Bones*? I brought him raisins and apples and cookies every morning so he wouldn't die."

Mrs. Redding appealed to Mom and Dad. "Look at him. Does he look like I've starved him?"

"Of course he doesn't." I was shouting now. "That's because he dug up some of his own money and bought himself food and clothes. What else could he do with a miser for a mother?"

"Caitlin," Dad said quietly, "I think you've made your point."

I shut up, but I was still steaming.

"Maybe you should put Edith to bed," Dad said to Mom.

I glanced back at Mrs. Redding. She seemed to be shriveling over her coffee cup.

Bones pushed away from the table. "I'll take her home."

"No," Mom said. "I think it would be better if you both slept here tonight."

"I can handle her." He went to his mother to help her out of her chair, but Dad stopped him with a hand on his shoulder.

"Paul, we wouldn't feel comfortable if you didn't

have someone with you. I know you're capable, but she might need more help then you can give her."

"All right," Bones agreed. "I'll call my aunt. She'll come over and stay with us."

I jumped up. "I'll show you where the phone is."

I waited in the living room while Bones called his aunt. When he hung up, he sat down on the davenport beside me. "She'll be right over."

"Good," I said. "I knew you wouldn't want to stay here."

He nodded and we sat together quietly until his aunt knocked on the front door. She was the efficient type. She asked Mom pointed questions about what happened, said she'd call the hospital to see if Bones needed a tetanus shot, and had Dad help them take Mrs. Redding home.

Up in bed, I kept seeing Bones's bloody white face each time I closed my eyes. To distract myself, I added up the diggings I'd heard. Mrs. Redding did the first one and the second one. Only the second time, Bones saw her bury the little can and he took the gold coin out of that. And then he watched her bury the next can, which was the fourth time I heard them. He started to dig that can up, too, but she caught him. Five diggings. And old Mr. Kager was right about Mrs. Redding buying the gold. I drifted off to sleep.

DURING breakfast, Dad said he thought Mom should see to it that Mrs. Redding went to a psychiatrist. Mom said she'd bring it up, but she thought Mrs. Redding's sister could be more convincing. While they were talking, I was thinking of Mr. Mitchell. I told them about the car phone and wires I'd seen in his bedroom.

Dad shook his head. "The Dorman kids wouldn't risk selling anything to an adult. Mr. Mitchell probably took the phone out of the box to try to install it himself and found out he couldn't."

That was probably true, I thought. I'd finished eating, so I offered to take Jimmy for a swing. Mom and Dad were pleased. They were left to read the Sunday paper in peace.

I saw to it that our back door made a bang and that the swing squeaked. I had to wait only a couple minutes before Bones came though the gate. He was barefoot. And wearing his new jeans, but that was all.

I slipped off the swing and put Jimmy in the grass near where Bones knelt. "How's your mom?" I asked him.

"Okay. My aunt's talking to her about going for counseling."

"She better. Dad says she needs a psychiatrist." I

153

pointed to the bandage on his forehead. "Does that hurt?"

"Not much."

"How did your mother get the shovel away from you anyway?"

"How do you think? I couldn't fight my *mom*."

"And another thing I've been wondering," I said. "How did you spend a gold coin?"

"I got an older guy to sell it."

"Bob Dorman!"

"I just gave him a cut to cash in the coin. I didn't do anything else with him."

"Oh, I didn't think you did," I said quickly. "But how were you going to exchange the new coin you were digging up? Get one of Bob's customers to do it?"

That was one too many questions for Bones. He was busy picking through a patch of clover.

"Here." He held out his hand to me, smiling. "Have a four leaf clover."

"Thanks," I said.

He got to his feet. "You can press it in one of those books you read."

As I watched him go back through the gate, I twirled the clover in my fingers. I'd press it in my photo album, I decided. That way I could keep it forever.